MATT JAFFE

The
Lovesick
Salesman

CASTLE

CANDY SHOP

KINGDOM OF CORIANDER

The Lovesick Salesman

Margaret Gray

illustrations by **Randy Cecil**

Henry Holt and Company · *New York*

Once again I would like to thank Reka Simonsen, the most talented and patient editor in the world. For their helpful comments on earlier drafts, I'm also grateful to John Altman, Harry Mittleman, and Ilene Silk's 2002–2003 class at the Crossroads School, Santa Monica.

Henry Holt and Company, LLC
Publishers since 1866
115 West 18th Street, New York, New York 10011
www.henryholt.com

Henry Holt is a registered trademark of Henry Holt and Company, LLC
Text copyright © 2004 by Margaret Gray
Illustrations copyright © 2004 by Randy Cecil
All rights reserved. Distributed in Canada by H. B. Fenn and Company Ltd.

Library of Congress Cataloging-in-Publication Data
Gray, Margaret
The lovesick salesman / Margaret Gray; illustrations by Randy Cecil.—1st ed.
p.   cm.
Summary: Even after being refused admission to the Heroic Academy,
Irwin, a lowly shopkeeper in the Kingdom of Coriander, longs to prove that
he is a true hero and win the love of the beautiful, wise Princess Julia.
ISBN-13: 978-0-8050-7558-8
ISBN-10: 0-8050-7558-5
[1. Fairy tales. 2. Heroes—Fiction. 3. Princesses—Fiction. 4. Knights and
knighthood—Fiction. 5. Humorous stories.] I. Cecil, Randy, ill. II. Title.
PZ8.G7495 Lo 2004   [Fic]—dc22   2003056980
First Edition—2004 / Book designed by Donna Mark
Printed in the United States of America on acid-free paper. ∞
1 3 5 7 9 10 8 6 4 2

For my parents,
who always believed in me,
usually against their better judgment

The
Lovesick
Salesman

Chapter 1

A very long time ago, when this morning's mud puddles were still vast oceans and dragons prowled their shores, there lived a little boy named Irwin who wanted to be a hero.

If you think he sounds too ambitious, you should remember that the young people of olden times felt more pressure to succeed than we do. Not only was history being made all around them, but the sense of limitation that prevents you and me from, say, turning into frogs or sleeping for hundreds of years hadn't been invented yet. Real people did those things, and even odder ones, every day, and the stories we call fairy tales were breaking news. So although children had more interesting career choices, they also had a lot to live up to.

The most popular celebrities of all were heroes, who walked the earth with mighty strides, slaying villains, righting wrongs, and setting hearts aflutter. Every little boy hoped for a job in that field, but only the Heroic Academy could confer a license, and it was ruthlessly selective.

Irwin planned to apply as soon as he was old enough—ten. Of course he knew the competition would be tough. All his friends looked a lot more heroic than he did: lean and bronzed, with curly hair and satin capes that flapped jauntily in the breeze. Irwin was simply too fond of candy to be lean; his skin wouldn't tan nor his hair curl; and his cape must have been cut wrong, because it just hung limp, even in strong wind. His demeanor, too, was less impressive than everybody else's. When his friends galloped their steeds across the hills, their jaws working with resolve and their steely eyes scanning the horizon, Irwin followed at a slower pace, chewing caramels. The one time he tried the most fashionable move of the day— leaping onto a rearing horse and thundering into the sunset—he pitched face first into a blackberry thicket.

But he wasn't as troubled by his shortcomings as everybody else seemed to be, and he didn't imagine that they would make any difference to the Academy. As long as his heart was pure, how could it matter that he sometimes slipped out of his saddle or had sugar on his chin? None of the other boys could resist his silly sense of humor or his generosity in sharing the candy his parents made in their shop. He'd even won over the most dashing boy in the entire kingdom, Seymour. Some of the others wondered jealously why Seymour didn't pick a best friend more like himself, a boy who would constantly try to outdo him and keep him at the top of his game. The truth was that, although Seymour seemed to accomplish everything effortlessly, it took all his strength to be that magnificent, and Irwin was the only person easygoing enough to help him forget the burden of his greatness.

Seymour was so impressive that the Academy had already offered him a spot in the next freshman class. Naturally, as his friends' auditions approached, Seymour was much in demand as a strategic consultant. Irwin didn't ask him for advice, but Seymour couldn't bear the idea of going to school without his friend and stayed up all night developing an application routine for him anyway.

He wrote it up on a parchment scroll and presented it proudly the next day as they ate caramels together in the shop. "It's been a challenge because you're deficient in most of the basics," he said, "but I think I've finally done it. For example—the opening gambit. It's usually best to gallop in on a charger, but you look so much like a sack of potatoes in the saddle that it would be counter-productive. Instead you'll stride in on foot, ringingly claiming to be greater than all the committee members put together."

Irwin handed the scroll back to him and laughed.

"*You* could say that, but it would sound ridiculous coming from me. I'm just going to open with a few jokes and then talk a little bit about the man who inspired me to be a hero."

Seymour groaned and clapped his hand to his forehead. "Not your favorite speech about Mortimer and true heroism?"

Irwin nodded. "Of course." Mortimer, the greatest hero of the era, had single-handedly beaten back the goblin hordes into the wastelands and the dragons into their mountain caves. But the real reason Irwin idolized him was that he avoided attention. Other champions made public appearances for extra income or showed off at heroic rallies, but Mortimer always refused such invitations, implying that until evil had been driven from the face of the earth, he couldn't spare the time. He seldom even waited around to be thanked. "Mortimer gives me hope that a person doesn't have to be a show-off to accomplish great things," added Irwin. "He's the only hero I've ever heard of who's not in it for the glory."

Seymour sighed. They'd had this argument before. "You can't be sure of that. His elusiveness doesn't hurt his business, after all. In fact, it's a clever strategy. When he finally makes an appearance, people will pay through the nose to see him. But in my opinion it's a cold and calculating way to go through life. Fans want to admire their heroes. *I'll* always be available to mine."

Irwin sometimes thought that Seymour was a little too interested in being admired and that he was letting his own personality color his view of Mortimer. "Have you ever considered that Mortimer just might not make a very good first impression? I'm sure that has something to do with why he's never rescued a princess. They're notoriously hard to please, and they probably make Mortimer feel awkward and shy."

Mortimer's perpetual bachelorhood was one of the most enticing mysteries about him. His fans didn't look forward to the day he would get distracted by lovey-dovey stuff and wedding arrangements, the way every other hero did, but they couldn't help wondering why it had never happened. Rescuing a princess usually led to marrying her, which meant retiring from active duty, and some people figured that Mortimer was too committed to his work to settle down. Still, it seemed odd that he'd never been tempted. Seymour believed that no princess had ever been good enough for Mortimer and that he was holding out for a real showstopper.

"But, Irwin, let's just say for the sake of argument that you're right," Seymour said after they'd debated for a while. "Mortimer's got a solid reputation in the field, so he can act however he wants. You're just a kid, and you still need to impress the committee. With my routine, specifically tailored to mask your flaws—"

"Thanks, Seymour," said Irwin, "but I really want to do it my way. Those professors are experts at detecting heroic qualities, and if I have them, they'll know it whether I try to show them off or not. And if not, it's better to find out now. I can always make caramel for a living, after all."

Seymour looked horrified at the suggestion, and Irwin wasn't nearly as lighthearted about it as he sounded, but he didn't really think it would happen. Among the hundreds of news stories published every year about people who transformed themselves dramatically in the pursuit of their dreams, there were always a few in which some unprepossessing person was rewarded for being himself.

Chapter 2

A few days later, Irwin stood facing the admissions committee of retired heroes—large, craggy men with flinty expressions. In the center sat the headmaster, Quentin the Hidebound, who was rumored to have been invincible in his youth and who still looked as though he'd put up a good fight.

"Hi!" Irwin said, with a little wave. "I'm Irwin, and I'm very grateful for the opportu—"

"We know who you are," interrupted Quentin, studying Irwin's application. "Let's see. . . ." Pausing, he flipped the page over. "You didn't list any exploits in section B as instructed." He looked up sharply. "A rebel,

eh?" He jotted a note. "Very good. Just boast to us a bit now."

"Er . . . ," said Irwin, "well, you see, I haven't actually performed any exploits yet."

"Of course you haven't!" boomed Quentin. "You're only ten! The point is to see how creative you are in inventing them. The whole first year at the Academy is devoted to boasting."

Irwin frowned. "But how can the students have anything to boast about in the first year?"

"Oh, they don't. That's why a vivid imagination is a prerequisite. Studies have shown that it's best to teach the mannerisms—the tone, inflection, gestures—of braggadocio early. Wait too long and modesty can set in. Even a working hero finds it necessary to exaggerate once in a while, so it helps to get the knack of it when you're young." Quentin checked the hourglass impatiently. "Go ahead, make something up. Borrow a feat from your favorite hero if you must."

Irwin tried to picture himself, only ten years old, beating back goblin hordes. The idea made him smile.

Quentin cleared his throat. "Perhaps a tankard of strong ale would steady your nerves?"

"I'm sorry," Irwin said. "It's just that I prepared some—"

Quentin cued a trumpet player Irwin hadn't noticed before, who let out a deafening blast. "Let's move on to your routine, then."

Irwin jumped. "Er," he began. He decided it would be best to skip the jokes and move straight into his main points. "Well, in my view, a true hero—"

"Stop the music!" interrupted Quentin. "All right, son, you're trying my patience. Are you ready to do your routine yet, or do you have something else to say?"

"But saying things *is* my routine. I prepared a brief monologue on the nature of true heroism."

Quentin stared at him. "The whole point of the audition is to see how impressive you are in motion. Do you want to get into this school or not?"

"Of course I do!" said Irwin. "But—"

"Then stop babbling and swagger!"

Irwin gulped. "But, the thing is, I—a true hero—"

"Swagger."

Irwin could tell from the glitter in Quentin's eyes that he meant business, and it would have taken a stronger will than his to resist such powerful charisma. The problem was that he couldn't swagger. He'd watched Seymour do it hundreds of times—his chin thrust out, his eyes steely, and his shoulders, eyebrows, elbows, and knees all working together in a complex but seamless rhythm— and he'd even tried it himself, but he'd always felt ridiculous. "The trick is to take yourself completely seriously," Seymour always said. "No smirking, no rolling your eyes. If you don't buy it, how will anybody else?" But Irwin couldn't help imagining that he looked like a monkey, and then Seymour would tell him he *did* look like one, and the practice session would end in laughter.

Things didn't seem so funny all of a sudden. He cracked his knuckles, breathed deeply, and took a step.

He immediately lost his balance and teetered on one foot, windmilling his arms. "Sorry," he muttered, regaining control and trying again. Although he managed to move forward this time, every part of him seemed to be at odds with another, his elbows competing with his eyebrows, his ankles undermining his knees, his hair falling in his eyes. One by one he brought each element in line, though, until he was surefooted enough to add a little hop.

"What are you doing?" demanded Quentin. "You look like a monkey. Chin up!"

But Irwin's chin wouldn't go any higher. His efforts to force it only made his eyes bulge.

"Now you look like a goose," snapped another committee member. "Toes out!"

"Back straight! Tummy flat! Waggle that rump! Come on, really swing it! Keep time! Elbows out! Elbows back in! Do-si-do! Eyebrows up! Eyebrows down!" The commands came faster and faster. Trying to follow them all at once, Irwin stumbled, did a somersault, and ended up cross-legged on the floor.

"Enough!" barked Quentin. He turned to the others, and they all put their heads together and whispered ferociously. Irwin got to his feet, wishing he hadn't let the pressure get to him. He should have refused to swagger and asked for a chance to explain. Maybe there was still time.

"Where to begin?" said Quentin at last. "Your attitude is not heroic at all. Heroes don't wave and say 'hi' upon entering a room. They glance swiftly at its occupants, quirking their left eyebrows to suggest that they don't think much of what they see. And heroes are not 'grateful for opportunities. . . .'" He rubbed the bridge of his nose. "But the real problem is that your ego seems to be very underdeveloped for your age. You could never keep up with the other boys."

"But why does ego matter?" said Irwin. "I know that boasting and swaggering—and the thing with the eyebrows—are impressive, but they're not necessary to doing good deeds, are they?"

Quentin sighed. "Maybe they weren't long ago, when the world was a more perilous place and people really needed help. But now, because of Mortimer and his generation, we're looking at a serious quest shortage. Most of our graduates will never encounter a villain or rescue a princess, at least not without waiting in a long line. Everybody wants a true hero, and these mannerisms are the only way to announce your qualifications. Without them you won't get work, and the Academy can't take that risk. We have a reputation to protect. Thank you." He crumpled up Irwin's application and threw it over his shoulder. "Next."

"A true hero—" began Irwin desperately, but his voice

was drowned out by hoofbeats as the next applicant came galloping in on a charger, sword raised, and nearly beheaded him. While he hurried out of the way, the committee rose as one man and offered this boy a full scholarship.

"Go right back there and boast your heart out," said Seymour when Irwin told him the sad news. "Tell them it was all a mistake. I can train you to swagger properly in five minutes, if you concentrate, and—"

"But it wasn't a mistake," said Irwin. "If that's what being a hero is all about, then I'm not cut out for it. Even if I could fake my way into the Academy, I wouldn't pass a single course." He put on a brave smile. "But don't be sad for me. I like caramel, after all. It's not a glorious career, but at least it brings people pleasure."

"But what am *I* supposed to do without you?" asked Seymour. "I'm liable to lose my sense of humor entirely."

"We can still be friends," Irwin said. "You can come by the shop in the afternoons, and I'll give you all the candy you can eat—unless you're on some wild-boar-shank-and-ale diet, of course."

Seymour smiled wanly at the joke. But they both had a feeling that things would never be the same.

Chapter 3

Irwin and Seymour lived in the Kingdom of Coriander, which was an extremely conventional place. Like all the best royal couples, King Virgil and Queen Marianne had three daughters. They paid most of their attention to the youngest, Julia, partly because of her extraordinary beauty and sweetness, but also because, moments after her birth, the older two, Mimi and Murgatroyd-Liza, had turned into wicked witches and flown away on broomsticks, vowing to return only on holidays.

19

Although Virgil and Marianne had expected this turn of events—it was tradition, after all—even they found the timing surprising. Beauty so infuriating to sisters usually took at least a year to develop, but already the newborn Julia was the most exquisite creature ever beheld. It was a bittersweet time for the family. The king and queen worried about the first two girls even as they looked forward to the triumphant wedding of the third. They were romantic people who'd enjoyed a famous courtship themselves—he'd rescued her from enchantment—and they expected nothing less than true love for Julia.

In the meantime, however, they weren't sure what to do with her, for they were very busy. The legend of their romance had spread to the four corners of the earth, and lovelorn people sent them questions. The king and queen wrote each back personally, in a firm, no-nonsense tone enlivened by tart humor that only increased the demand for their advice. They spent most of their time abroad at conferences on matters of the heart, putting the king-dom in the hands of the wise men and leaving their daughter on her own.

Luckily, Julia was as resourceful as she was pretty. Knowing that her parents trusted her to bring herself up well, she took her job seriously, consulting history books and child-rearing manuals and assigning her own educational play. She even built a dollhouse for her sixth birthday, a replica of the Coriander castle down to the gargoyles, and pretended to be surprised when she found it wrapped up with a ribbon next to the nutritious breakfast she'd cooked.

The wise men were another story. They ran things all right at first, but after a while they got bored with the dreary paperwork and started taking long lunches and leaving early for the day. The kingdom slid into decline. Within a few years the flying buttresses landed, the public square grew choked with weeds, the statue of the king in princely splendor lost its nose, spiders made their

home in the armory, and the ledger where the tax records had once been carefully kept lay under an inch of dust.

Only Julia seemed to notice. She wondered why she spent all her time polishing the tiny silver in her doll kingdom when the real one needed her help. So one day, when the wise men ambled into the office at midmorning, they found the little princess waiting. What she said to them has been lost to history, but a few days later the buttresses were back in flight, the square was freshly cobbled, the marble king's nose was restored (more aquiline than ever), the treasury was replenished, and the armory sparkled with enough weapons for a ten years' war—although Julia's foreign policy was so benign and cautious that things never went that far.

By her twelfth birthday, she'd gotten good enough at running the government that she had time on her hands once again, and sometimes she found herself staring through her window at the children who played out in the square. Traditionally, princesses didn't associate with commoners and went outdoors only on litters, so her longing to join them took her by surprise. Was it possible that she was lonely? What could she do about it? She didn't know any other children. Her sisters, who still came home on holidays, had long since grown up, and they were so wicked that she'd never felt close to them. After some research, she determined that a pet would help.

There were no pet shops in olden times, but some animals, believing domestic life to be more pleasant than survival of the fittest, took the initiative and made themselves available for taming in the woods. Julia's problem was how to get there. If she wanted to go out, she was supposed to make a reservation with the litter service several weeks in advance, declare a national holiday to ensure that the streets would be empty, and take along an entire retinue and three-piece orchestra. What a headache it would be, and all the drama would surely put off even the friendliest animals.

She decided to skip all that and go alone in disguise. If her parents had been around, she never would have entertained this notion, but having absolute power had made her a little headstrong. She found an old suit of armor— very unfashionable, a gaudy shade of gold, with wide chain-mail lapels—in one of the downstairs closets. It was too big for her. Her head didn't even reach the collar, so the empty helmet flopped from side to side, and she had to prop it up with one arm, squinting to see through a buttonhole as she staggered along in the enormous boots. But at least she didn't look like a princess in it.

She arranged for two notoriously sleepy palace guards to be on duty on Tuesday afternoons and for a heavy lunch to be served before their shift. It worked perfectly. Nobody paid any attention to the quaint knight who, bonging like an empty kettle with every step, walked right past the snoring guards and into the world.

Chapter 4

That very afternoon, Irwin and Seymour set out for a walk in the Coriander woods. They were both fifteen years old by now, and were still the best of friends. Their differences had grown so pronounced over the years, though, that they made an odd couple. Irwin was round, a little stooped, and spattered with sugar syrup from his work at the candy shop, where he was now the evening manager. Although he had a pleasant face and an appealing, gently humorous gleam in his eye, few people looked at him long enough to notice.

Seymour, in contrast, had grown into a truly outstanding young man. His massive, craggy face could have been carved by a powerful force of nature. His shoulders were broad, his strawberry-blond hair was the ideal texture for whipping in strong winds, and his glance was unsettlingly keen. These traits, along with his gleaming white smile, conspired to make him the center of attention wherever he went.

But he wasn't smiling that day. The ground quaked under his impatient tread, and his broad brow was furrowed. "Imagine the gall of Professor Voldo, insisting that we provide *proof*," he fumed. "There simply aren't any real exploits left to perform. That's why we're forced to make them up."

Irwin nodded sympathetically. Seymour had kept him up to date about the problems at the Academy. The quest shortage had worsened over the years, finally becoming an international crisis. The wastelands and swamps where only the mightiest had formerly dared to venture now crawled with young men looking for wrongs to right and squabbling over the minor annoyances they did scrounge up. The once-lonely trails to the dragon caves were constantly jammed with grouchy heroes on rearing steeds. Every kingdom had its share of unemployed champions who loitered in the streets, smelling of strong ale and boasting to anybody who'd listen about how well they'd done at heroism school.

Naturally some had questioned the Academy's standards, and the Heroic Certification Board had conducted an audit, concluding after months of investigation that the students were *too* creative; it was impossible to tell anymore who was a real hero and who wasn't. Now Seymour and his schoolfellows, so good at inventing accomplishments, were being forced to provide evidence.

Irwin didn't think this change was necessarily bad—it couldn't hurt Seymour to get some hands-on experience—but he hated to see his friend unhappy.

"I could go and tell your professor that you spend time with me every day," he suggested after a while. "That's a good deed. It shows your loyalty, your generosity, your kindness—"

Seymour snorted. "Thanks, but a feat like *that* isn't going to get me into any legends. Anyway, he already wonders why my papers always have caramel on them, and he might figure out that I let you do my homework for me."

"Only the parts that don't require any charisma," said Irwin. "But, you know, I've been thinking. As much as I enjoy your homework, maybe I'm not doing you any favors by— What on earth is that?" A cacophonous rattle filled the air. Irwin looked around to see a knight in

golden armor tumbling down the riverbank into the rushing waters below. "Seymour, quick!" he cried, setting off at a run.

Seymour's brow cleared, and he whipped a small notebook out of his vest pocket. "This ought to satisfy Voldo. Rescue of knight in golden armor, 4 P.M., Tuesday. Witness: Irwin. I'll get the knight's name after I've carried him free of the waters. . . . Hmmm, that reminds me. These are new crushed-velvet knee breeches." He bent down and carefully rolled them up, adjusting each cuff until it brimmed just so over his boots.

Irwin, meanwhile, had splashed into the river, pulled the knight to safety, and set him on his feet. The stranger's helmet lolled loosely from side to side, and spluttering noises emerged from his chest.

"I hope we're not too late," said Irwin worriedly. "Seymour?" He looked around, noticing for the first time that his friend wasn't with him.

Seymour appeared above the riverbank, tucked his notebook in his pocket, and climbed down in one step. Pushing past Irwin, he seized the knight by the shoulders and peered through his visor. "No sign of life. Oh, cursed fate, to snatch him so untimely from my grasp!"

Inside the armor, Julia coughed and gasped. She

blinked the last of the water out of her eyes and peered out the buttonhole to see where she'd ended up—and who'd become so vehemently involved in her welfare.

The most magnificent boy she'd ever seen was standing before her. She had to press her eye to the buttonhole and look upward to take in all of him, but the view was worth the effort. It wasn't just his rough-hewn features, or the way the late-afternoon sun shone through his strawberry-blond ringlets, that melted her heart—it was the look of desperate concern in his keen eyes. He'd saved her life! He didn't know her, had never even seen her face, and yet he seemed to have such a stake in her survival. She'd never dreamed a person could be so honorable. "Er . . . I'm all right," she managed at last in a small voice, which nonetheless echoed in the cavernous armor, making the boys jump. "Thanks to you."

"Think nothing of it," said Seymour, taking out his notebook again. "Now if you wouldn't mind answering a few questions for purposes of authentication. You are?"

"Ah . . . ," said Julia, who hadn't expected to talk to anybody and hadn't thought about her cover story. "My name is . . . um . . . Sir . . . Bildungs . . . roman. From the . . . er . . . Kingdom of Fffff . . ." She trailed off, too dazed to think of a good way to end the word.

But Seymour was scribbling in his notebook. "Four Fs or five? Oh, who cares? The secretaries can fill that part in. Let's see . . . well, if this gets made into a legend, it helps to have a little more background on you. Could you tell me what brought you here today?"

"Oh! The raven!" exclaimed Julia, pointing toward the riverbank. "There, under that tree, sick and shivering. I was going to take him home, nurse him back to health, and make a pet of him, but it's a little slippery, and these are new boots."

Seymour couldn't resist casting a skeptical glance at the rusty boots before turning to look behind him. Irwin stood on the riverbank cradling a bird. Seymour plucked the creature out of his friend's arms and held it out to the knight. "Is this the raven you mean?"

"Oh, thank you!" cried Julia. Reaching for it, she let go of her helmet, which flopped so far to the side that it fell off and thudded to the ground. Her hands flew to the empty space above her collar. Mortified, she dropped to her knees and patted the ground.

Seymour, still holding the bird, was trying to write in

his notebook. "Again, it's second nature to me," he murmured. "Now, you'll just need to sign here, and then I'll start a new entry for the rescue of the bird. Two feats in one day, Irwin. Voldo will never believe it."

"Er, Seymour," said Irwin nervously.

"Oh, good thinking," said Seymour. "I probably *should* show him to Voldo, since a bird can't sign its name. Sir Bildungsroman, would you mind lending me your raven for a few hours—" He looked up, around, and finally down. "Good grief! A headless knight! The most fearsome of all foes! We just did a unit on them. Hold these, Irwin. I'm going to need both hands." He gave the bird and the notebook to Irwin. "And while you're at it, start a new entry: Slaying headless knight." He pulled out his sword and snicked it through the air.

"Wait!" cried Julia, still on her knees. "I'm not a headless knight!"

"Just as Voldo said: They always deny being headless," Seymour told Irwin. "I'll believe *that* when I see your head, foul fiend!"

As Seymour towered above her with his sword raised, Julia managed to spring the latch on the side of her armor. Its two halves popped apart, and she tumbled out at his feet like a beautiful tousled baby bird.

Chapter 5

"I can explain," said Julia, scrambling to her feet and brushing leaves off her finery. But she paused, thinking how irresponsible it had been to leave the palace. Worse still, she'd compromised her dignity in the eyes of this wonderful boy—and his silly-looking companion, whom she noticed for the first time.

Irwin *was* staring at her in a slack-jawed and dopey way, but it wasn't entirely his fault. Julia's beauty could undo people who'd known her for years, and he hadn't been prepared. He felt the uncharacteristic impulse to compare parts of her face to natural phenomena. "Eyes as black as the night sky," he muttered. "Hair in waves like the storm-tossed sea . . ."

Seymour, on the other hand, had gone through two years of resistance training to immunize himself against just such reactions, so he could turn on the charm even when taken aback. He sheathed his sword and bowed low before the princess. "Your Majesty," he intoned suavely. "I recognize your exquisite visage from the coins of the realm, although no carving could do it justice. I am Seymour the Ideal, and this is my loyal steward. Irwin, give the princess her bird. Ahem. Irwin?"

Irwin jumped to attention. "Oh, sorry, er . . . Master," he said. He bowed and handed the raven to Julia with trembling hands.

Julia barely noticed him. "How kind," she breathed to Seymour. "But are you sure you wouldn't like to keep him? You're the one who rescued him, after all, and didn't you say you needed him?"

"Nonsense," said Seymour. "I'm sure Irwin will corroborate my story, although that Voldo *is* a tough audience. . . ."

Julia heard the bell that meant her afternoon staff meeting was about to begin. She didn't want to be late—she was trying to institute a land reform, which the wise men would use any excuse to squash—but she hated to run off without finding a way to see Seymour again. "Please do borrow him," she said impulsively. "I know you'll treat him gently during his convalescence. If he recovers and you can bear to part with him, you can return him to me in one week's time, in the same place." She gave the raven a last kiss and handed him to Seymour. Then, buckling up her armor and reattaching the way-ward helmet, she bonged away through the trees.

Seymour transferred the raven to Irwin with a distasteful expression. "Ugh," he said, wiping his hands on his snow-white handkerchief. "Obviously riddled with disease."

Irwin stroked the bird's head. "I think he just has a little cold. He'll recover in no time, especially if his reward is to be Julia's pet. What strange and wonderful fortune it is that we met her."

"I know! A solid day's work at last!" agreed Seymour, flipping his notebook open. "Too bad I can't tell Voldo I rescued her, but Sir Bildungsroman makes almost as good a story, and anyway I'm laying the groundwork for a real achievement, if you know what I mean. I get the sense the kid likes me, and she won't be bad-looking in a few years. Prince Seymour the Ideal has a nice ring to it, don't you think?"

Wrapping the bird in his handkerchief, Irwin suppressed a twinge of envy. Seymour was right, of course. Julia was obviously smitten with him, and the story of how he'd rescued her and the raven was romantic, even if it wasn't exactly true. This sort of thing was happening more and more often. Seymour looked so perfect that people automatically gave him credit for doing noble things, and he accepted their praise whether he deserved it or not. Irwin didn't really mind that Seymour cheated on his homework—the Academy professors should be harder to fool—but it didn't seem right to deceive a lovely person like Julia. If she knew who had *really* rescued her— Oh, who was he kidding? She'd still have eyes only for Seymour.

As he often did when he felt uncomfortable, he made a joke. "Sure, Prince Seymour sounds good, but not as magnificent as Irwin the Steward."

Seymour shot him an irritable glance. "Look, I'm sorry about that steward business. You don't mind, do you? After all, maybe you *can* be my steward someday. When I'm prince I can afford to hire you!"

"Just as long as you make me polish your boots and clean out the stables," said Irwin. "And give me forty lashes whenever I'm late."

"Hmmph," sniffed Seymour. "Some humble caramel shopkeepers would be grateful for the patronage of the future prince of Coriander."

"Oh, Seymour, you know I'm grateful for everything you do for me," Irwin apologized, a little sadly, for he remembered a time when his friend would have laughed at his joke. Had the Academy destroyed Seymour's sense of fun entirely?

"I'm beginning to wonder about that," said Seymour. "If you *really* want to make it up to me, you can take care of that bird, after I use it to prove my accomplishment to Voldo, of course."

The raven made a big hit at the Academy, where the story of Seymour's double rescue quickly became a legend. Even though none of the professors knew exactly where Fffff was, and this Sir Bildungsroman character sounded a little too good to be true, they were so relieved that one of their students had performed certifiable feats that they didn't ask too many questions. They began to speak of Seymour as their greatest hope, the one student who could restore their profession to its former glory.

Irwin took the bird home, where he fed him a steady diet of caramels and named him Richard. He grew so fond of him that he regretted having to return him to the princess when the time came. It was some consolation that she seemed delighted by his recovery—even though she credited Seymour wholly with the accomplishment.

"Aw, it was nothing. I'll miss the little fellow," said Seymour, chucking the raven patronizingly under the beak.

Julia looked moved. "Maybe you should keep him, especially now that you've nursed him back to health."

"Oh, no," said Seymour, masterfully concealing his alarm with increased courtliness. "I did it for you. He's yours, really."

"Are you sure? He's used to you, and maybe—"

Irwin stepped in. "Since you both have a claim on his affection, maybe you should share custody. You could each keep him for a week at a time. You could meet next Tuesday, for example, and Seymour could take him, and so on."

Both agreed to the idea—Julia with particular enthusiasm—but on the way home Seymour said to Irwin, "What's gotten into you? Couldn't you think of some way for us to meet without involving that mangy beast? You'll just have to take care of him during my weeks."

Irwin was delighted to spend more time with Richard, who had turned out to be a charming conversationalist. And it wasn't often he met somebody who liked caramels as much as he did.

Chapter 6

For Julia, the months that followed were both wonderful and terrible. She'd never known what it was like to have friends, so she looked forward all week to seeing them—especially Seymour. At first, actually, she thought only about Seymour, and if anybody had asked her about Irwin, she would have had a hard time placing the name. But after a while, observing how fond Richard seemed of him, she began to warm up to him. She saw what a devoted steward he was, and how his self-deprecating jokes could lighten Seymour's grimmest mood. They put her at ease, too—or at least as close to ease as she could get when Seymour was around.

For although she admired Seymour more each time she saw him, she feared that he didn't feel the same way about her. The novelty of embarrassing her with courtly phrases had already worn off. Now he spent their time together demonstrating flourishes, war whoops, devastating backward glances while riding into the jaws of peril, and other highlights from his heroic repertoire as she, Irwin, and Richard looked admiringly on. Even when he wasn't performing, it was obvious that he thought she was just a silly kid. And who could blame him? She always acted dopey around him. She lay awake at night thinking up clever remarks, but in his presence, she—the shadow ruler of Coriander, all cool-headed efficiency before the wise men—could do nothing except blush.

Every week she hoped he would show some little sign of true love, but instead he only grew more restless, hurrying back ever more eagerly to school. He was learning to joust, and talking about it put the kind of fire in his eyes that Julia longed to kindle. She became so moody and inattentive that the wise men were able to reverse most of her reforms, and Coriander historians later called this period a miniature dark age.

She'd never paid much attention before to her parents' work, and now that she could have used their expertise, they were away on business for most of the year. When they finally returned, Julia hurried to see them in the throne room. It was filled floor to ceiling with the letters they'd received in their absence, and the two of them sat like islands in a sea of white, scribbling as fast as they could on scented stationery.

"How about this?" King Virgil was saying as he held up a letter in progress. "'Dear Beast Missing His Beauty: Well, what did you expect? Not even a magic castle can replace a true emotional connection. If you really want her back, be honest about your identity.'"

The queen nodded thoughtfully. "Very true, dear. Listen to this one. 'Dear Had It with the Hi-Hos: Maybe if you were more cheerful, your fiancée wouldn't *want* to spend so much time with those dwarves. At least *they* whistle while they work.'"

Julia picked up a letter from the stack and pretended to read it. "Here's an interesting problem," she said. "This girl likes a certain boy, who's good at everything and who loves challenges, and she wants to know how to make him notice her."

"This is your territory, Marianne," said King Virgil with a wink.

The queen preened at the compliment. "Your father always gives me the easy ones. This girl's already answered her own question. All she needs to do is become his greatest challenge."

"How would I . . . er . . . she do that?" asked Julia. "She can't joust or—"

"Oh, my heavens, nothing like that. There are plenty of subtle feminine ways to be challenging. My technique was to be asleep when your father hacked his way through the briar bush that surrounded my enchanted kingdom. But she wouldn't have to go to that length. She could just act cold and unimpressed—play hard to get. By the way, honey, your sisters are coming home for a long weekend, so make sure you hide your cosmetics. They *will* make potions with them."

Julia nodded, but her brain was spinning. The next Tuesday she set out for the forest planning to ignore Seymour and talk the whole time to Irwin. If her mother was right, Seymour would declare undying devotion by the end of the afternoon. She got to the meeting place early, unlatched her Sir Bildungsroman suit and leaned it against a tree, and arranged herself in a nonchalant pose on a fallen log, not even looking in the direction of the Academy. After a long time she had a crick in her neck, and there was still no sign of Seymour.

"One quick look—just to make sure he's on his way—probably wouldn't spoil the effect," she reasoned. She scanned the empty woods and then went back to being indifferent.

A few minutes later a terrible thought occurred to her. "What if he sees me from a distance and thinks I look so unfriendly that he decides to go back home? Maybe I should wait until he gets here to put the plan in action."

Soon she was standing on tiptoe, wringing her hands and peering anxiously through the twilight.

Chapter 7

Irwin was waiting, too, outside the school where he usually met Seymour. His friend had never been late before, and he was worrying that some harm had befallen him, when suddenly he heard a roar of applause. He knew only one person capable of inspiring such enthusiasm. He followed the noise to the practice coliseum, where, sure enough, he discovered Seymour triumphantly jousting before an audience of underclassmen.

Seymour was already the best jouster at school. As Irwin looked on, he effortlessly unhorsed a dozen opponents, then stood on his saddle and waved to the crowd while his steed circled the stadium. Only after the entire audience had gone in to dinner did he dismount and stride to the sidelines to quaff a tankard of strong ale. He looked surprised to see Irwin waiting at the dispenser.

"Oh, is it Tuesday again?" he asked. "I'm afraid you'll have to go alone today. Charles and Philip invited me to carouse with them. Actually I'll probably be carousing every evening from now on, so you might let Julia know not to expect me anymore. People like heroes who work hard and play hard, too, and I need to solidify my reputation as the life of the party."

"But what about your dream of marrying Julia and ruling the kingdom someday?" asked Irwin. "Shouldn't that be your top priority?"

Seymour waved his hand dismissively. "I used to think ruling this dinky kingdom would be a good career, but I've realized it would stifle a man of my talents. I'm after worldwide recognition, the sort of fame that Mortimer has and doesn't even appreciate. I need to spend this time with other professionals in my field, not little girls."

"Little girls!" cried Irwin. "Julia may be young, but she's so beautiful and noble that I can't think of a greater accomplishment than winning her hand."

Seymour shrugged. "Oh, Irwin, you're so naive. Julia's

not the only princess in the world. I'd like to meet a few others before I make a commitment. And even if I decide later that I really do like Julia best, a little time off won't make any difference to her. She's so moony about me that she makes me nervous. I can just see the kind of wife she'll be—demanding all a man's attention, refusing to let him have any fun with the guys."

Irwin knew that Seymour responded better to jokes than to lectures, but he was too upset to be funny. "I had a feeling you didn't give Julia her due," he said coldly, "but I never suspected you of being so thickheaded. You should strive every day to deserve her good opinion. I can't believe you'd throw it away for some ale."

Seymour rolled his eyes and refilled his tankard. "Irwin, you've turned into a real goody-goody. At least Charles and Philip know how to have fun. They always ask me why I bother with a lowly caramel salesman, and I always explain that you make me laugh. But lately all you've done is lecture and judge. Maybe it's time we admitted that we don't have anything in common anymore, and there's no point in prolonging this childish acquaintance."

"Fine," said Irwin, turning away before Seymour could see the tears in his eyes.

Irwin headed for the woods alone, dreading telling Julia the grim news. He saw her standing alone in the forest, staring hopefully in his direction. The moment she recognized him, her shoulders sagged.

"Seymour's been . . . um . . . unavoidably detained," he murmured as he drew near.

Julia looked down, blinking and biting her lip. "I understand," she said. "He has better things to do than hang around with a silly girl."

"There's nothing better!" Irwin protested. "And you're not silly. Seymour's just, well, he's young, hasn't got his priorities straight yet."

"It's nice of you to lie to me, dear Irwin," said Julia. "But I know I just don't provide the sort of challenge that would interest a true hero. I try, honestly—"

Irwin was staring at her. "True hero? Seymour's just a teenage boy. He's better looking and more agile than most people, but he's got a long way to go before he'll be a true hero. Mortimer would—"

"I can't believe what I'm hearing," Julia interrupted. "You're always praising Seymour when he's here. The second he turns his back, you insult him. What kind of steward are you?"

"In the first place, I'm not his steward," said Irwin. He sighed, relieved to have gotten the truth off his chest. "I'm just his friend."

Julia's jaw dropped. "That makes it even worse. Some friend!"

"I want to be a good one," said Irwin. "He's always been generous to me, and even though we've had our disagreements lately, I'd never say a word against him to anyone else. But I can't stand the thought that you blame yourself for his selfish, insensitive—"

Julia held up her hand. "Enough! I won't hear it. And I won't be *your* friend anymore unless you take it back. Richard surely knows his way between the castle and

51

Seymour's house, so there's no need for us to see each other at all." She looked at him pleadingly. "But I would miss you. So just say Seymour is a true hero, and we'll forget this ever happened, okay?"

"I'm afraid I can't do that," said Irwin regretfully. "Mortimer is the only person I can call a true hero."

They stared at each other. Richard, on Julia's shoulder, looked back and forth between them. Just as it seemed the silence would stretch on forever, a strangled shout shattered it. They looked over to see a young man on horseback goggling at them through the gloom.

Irwin had gotten adjusted to Julia's beauty over the months, but he'd never forgotten the trauma of seeing it for the first time, and since then she'd grown even lovelier. The newcomer was obviously having a terrible reaction. He boasted for a few seconds in a hysterical babble before passing out in the underbrush.

After that the word was out, and heroes from miles around galloped in to wait beneath Julia's balcony. They stayed night and day, and they paid the staff to report her every gesture, so she couldn't have sneaked out even if she'd wanted to. Sir Bildungsroman languished in her bedroom closet. Richard commuted by wing between his two homes. Julia was often tempted to send a note

with him to Seymour, but she always remembered her mother's advice in the nick of time. Instead she threw herself into governing the kingdom. In a few months she'd made it once again the most enlightened realm in history, forcing the wise men into an ignominious retreat. But she had no power over her own heartache. Every evening she stepped out on her balcony to see if Seymour had come.

Whenever she did, her suitors went into action. They leaped on the backs of rearing steeds, jousted, dueled, swaggered, and boasted to the point of nervous exhaustion. Julia knew what it was like to love somebody whose mind was elsewhere, and she did her best to admire them. But having been spoiled by the perfection of Seymour's routines, she always noticed flaws in theirs—an eyebrow out of sync, a do-si-do late—and she couldn't help offering constructive criticism, which the heroes, understandably, took badly.

"What will it take to melt her icy heart?" they wondered, swallowing draughts of strong ale and redoubling their efforts. Soon she had a reputation as the most challenging princess in the land, inflaming the competitive spirit of thousands. Still, day after day, Seymour didn't appear.

Chapter 8

Irwin also kept busy at the shop. For days on end he thought of, and ate, nothing but caramel. Occasionally, as he stirred a simmering cauldron, he indulged in one of his boyish fantasies about breaking an enchantment or rescuing Julia from peril—but for the most part he was satisfied with his slow, sticky life. Three years passed. If it hadn't been for Richard, who faithfully spent alternate weeks with him, Irwin might have wondered if his friendship with Seymour and Julia had been a dream.

Then one afternoon the front door jangled. Wiping his sugary hands on his apron, he came out of the stock-room to see Seymour looming before him, enormous and stony as a cathedral.

Irwin was delighted, but he didn't want to seem too soft. "Good afternoon. Is there something I can help you with?" he asked stiffly.

Seymour seemed just as uncomfortable. "Yes, I'm looking for a few little things to give as graduation presents. You . . . er . . . might have heard I'm graduating tomorrow?"

"Oh, already?" Irwin asked. If things had gone differently all those years ago, it could have been *his* graduation, too. But there was no time to waste on regrets. He had a customer. He nimbly spread an array of tempting treats on the counter. "We have a selection of gift boxes. . . ."

Seymour listened for a few moments before bursting out, "Oh, hang it all, Irwin—I'll take a box, but the real reason I came by was to see if you'd like to come to the ceremony tomorrow. You were always a good friend to me, and it would mean a lot to me if you'd be there."

Irwin's pride melted. "If this was your way of getting free candy, it worked," he said, pushing all the samples across the counter. "Seriously, I'd be honored. What time? We're doing inventory tomorrow, but I can take an hour for lunch."

Seymour, beaming, shook his head. "You'll have to take off the whole afternoon if you want to hear the commencement address. You'll never guess who's giving it! I was going to save it as a surprise, but just to tempt you I'll tell you: the perfect hero, Mortimer. Didn't you kind of look up to him years ago?"

Irwin dropped a heavy cake of marzipan on his foot. "Mortimer?" he cried. "Mortimer's actually appearing in public? I thought he never did that."

"He's making an exception. This year's graduates are said to be the finest the Academy has ever produced— thanks to yours truly, of course—and I guess his curiosity got the better of him. But we don't know exactly what time he'll be there. He travels under darkest secrecy to avoid capture."

Irwin looked surprised. "Maybe I'm really out of touch, but the last I heard there were no villains left."

Seymour shook his head. "No, you're right. Mortimer has nothing to fear from traditional bad guys. It's the princesses he needs to watch out for."

"Princesses?" repeated Irwin.

"Not to mention duchesses, viscountesses, scullery maids, nuns, and, even more scandalously, a few queens, too. Every woman in the world wants to be rescued by a true hero, so when they hear he's in town they pretend to be trapped in towers or mistreated by stepmothers. He can't hear of anybody in peril without attempting a rescue, and they say he very nearly fell for more than one of these frauds. You can imagine how embarrassing it would be to end his career on such a note. Oh, speaking of princesses," Seymour added, as he swung open the door, "do you keep up with Julia?"

Irwin shook his head. "No. We haven't spoken since the last time you and I did—three years ago."

Seymour sighed. "Everybody says she's grown up into something special, but I've been too ashamed of the way I acted to go see her myself, and now it's too late."

"It's never too late to apologize," cried Irwin.

Seymour blinked at him. "No, I mean there isn't time. I'm heading off on my first quest the day after graduation, and who knows if I'll ever return?" He looked nobly off into the distance.

Irwin imagined rearing steeds, clashing swords, and barren towers rising against a bleak sky. How romantic and perilous Seymour's life would be! "What kind of quest?" he asked wistfully.

Seymour's face sagged a little. "Well—it's not exactly what we used to talk about when we were kids. The quest shortage is worse than ever, and the best thing I could find was a little feat up north. A duke there has an ant problem." He winced at Irwin's startled expression. "Would you believe I beat out fifty thousand applicants for the post? Still, everybody has to start somewhere. Rumor has it that the villains are licking their wounds and gathering strength, vowing to make the world cruel once again." He sighed. "I can only pray that they will— and soon. Well, I hope I'll see you tomorrow." The door jangled again and he was gone.

Irwin stood thinking for a moment. Then he took off his apron, put up the closed sign, and hurried to the public square. He'd avoided the place for years, hearing the rumors of how crowded it had gotten, but nothing could have prepared him for the spectacle that greeted him. Hundreds of heroes filled it, some on horseback, some on the cobblestones, all in various stages of love-sickness. It was obvious which of them had been there the longest by the way they slumped in glassy-eyed despair, while the newer arrivals still swaggered and boasted with unblemished hope. Vendors hawked ale and capes, and the air was smoky from the wild boars being slow-roasted over open fires.

Irwin threaded his way to stand beneath the princess's balcony, which sagged with flowers her admirers had thrown up to her. "Julia!" he hissed.

A hero with an official air appeared at his elbow. "Hey, what are you doing?" he asked. "You can't just waltz up and try to get the princess's attention. Put your name at the bottom of this list, and when it's your turn, we'll call you." He handed Irwin a heavy scroll.

Irwin staggered under the weight of it. "How long will it take?" he asked.

"We're looking at a three-year wait at this point," said the hero. "Julia hears ten pitches on a good day, but not even that makes a real dent."

"I can't wait three years!" exclaimed Irwin. "I have something very important to tell her, something I'm sure she'll want to know."

"We all do. Save it for your turn, buddy," said the hero.

Irwin signed the scroll, but as soon as the hero had disappeared again into the crowd, he tried again: "Julia!"

"Whoa!" Immediately the hero was back at his side. "What gives?"

Others rushed to weigh in on the controversy, which soon got so noisy with boasts, threats, and challenges that Julia came huffing out onto the balcony. "Boys, boys!" she shouted.

"Now you've done it," muttered the bossy hero.

"You promised to keep order out here, Leopold," said Julia reproachfully. "You know impressing hours don't start until four-thirty."

"It's not my fault," sulked Leopold. "It's *this* character here. He's trying to sneak ahead of everybody."

Julia looked at Irwin. "That's not very nice," she said. "You'll never impress me if you don't follow the rules."

"Your Majesty, I couldn't impress you if I followed every rule ever written," said Irwin with a wry smile.

Julia did a double take, and her face lit up. "Irwin?" she asked joyfully. "It's okay, Leopold. He's an old friend."

But as soon as Leopold had backed away, keeping a watchful eye on the newcomer, Julia's manner cooled. "Well, you *used* to be my friend. Richard isn't due back to Seymour until Tuesday, is he?"

"It's nothing to do with Richard," said Irwin. "I haven't forgotten the condition you set the last time we spoke. You'll be glad to know that although I can't quite declare Seymour a true hero yet, I *can* say that he's well on his way." He looked up at her earnestly. "Is that enough to make amends?"

Julia beamed so radiantly that hundreds of heroes in the crowd clutched their hearts and dropped to the cobblestones, and Irwin, too, felt unsteady. "It's almost exactly what I wanted to hear," she said, "and I'm so happy to see

you that I'll gladly accept it. Was it just time that changed your mind?"

Irwin shook his head. "No. He apologized about the way he'd behaved toward you years ago and said he felt too guilty about it to come himself. A true hero, of course, wouldn't have let that stop him, but at least he had the impulse."

Julia clasped her hands together. Seymour cared about her! He'd cared about her all along! He was afraid that *she* was mad at *him*. She'd come up with these explanations herself, many times, but she'd never quite believed them. "But of course I forgive him," she cried. "Tell him to come by tomorrow, if he's free."

Irwin shook his head. "He's graduating tomorrow, and then he's going off on a quest. He's invited me to the ceremony. And guess who'll be there? Mortimer!"

"Hmmm?" asked Julia distractedly, crestfallen. Seymour was leaving? All this time wasted on hurt pride, and now she might not see him for years, or ever again.

"If you could only see Mortimer, you'd understand why my standards are so high," Irwin was going on.

"I wish I could," said Julia absently.

"Can't you?" asked Irwin. "Maybe this is a job for Sir Bildungsroman!"

Julia gestured sadly at the heroes. "They watch me night and day."

"They never sleep?" Irwin asked, looking around at Leopold, who was glaring at him.

"They do it in shifts."

Irwin couldn't resist winking at Leopold, who turned red with thwarted rage and shook a fist at him. He turned back to Julia with a mischievous grin. "What if I created a disturbance? I could come by first thing in the morning and serenade you. While Leopold and the others are putting me in my place, Sir B. can slip out unnoticed."

"That might work," said Julia. "They do seem to dislike you so. But are you sure you don't mind going to all that trouble?"

"I'd do a lot more than that to see Sir Bildungsroman again," said Irwin.

After he got home, though, he wondered if he'd done the right thing. The moment Julia saw Mortimer, she was bound to fall in love with him. They were the most perfect beings on earth, obviously made for each other. He only hoped Seymour wouldn't be too disappointed.

Chapter 9

The next morning Irwin returned to Julia's balcony at dawn and broke into song. He'd compared the princess's features to so many natural phenomena over the years that he'd run out. As a result, his serenade dealt with unconventional subject matter: "Julia, you are so resourceful and competent! You understand tax laws and can balance a budget! You are the most enlightened shadow ruler in history, who looks out for the needy and downtrodden. How I love you for your intelligence and your devotion to your populace, the land reforms you have instituted and the serfs you have freed—"

Leopold, appearing with his customary swiftness, clapped a hand over Irwin's mouth.

"You again!" he growled. "I knew you were up to no good, but I never thought you'd pull something like this." He turned and waved the other suitors over. "He's trying to serenade her without any backup singers, using uncertified lyrics, at an unscheduled time."

In the thick of the ensuing squabble, the scullery door opened, and Sir Bildungsroman sidled out, with Richard on his shoulder. Irwin gave him a chance to blend in with the crowd before he made his apologies to Leopold and the others, handed out caramels, and hurried to catch up. The heroes yelled at his back, but their threats suddenly sounded sticky and unpersuasive.

"That was an unusual serenade," Julia remarked as they left the public square behind. "I'm not sure I've heard it before."

"Oh, just a little ditty off the top of my head," said Irwin lightly.

"You mean you wrote it?" asked Julia. "But it was so detailed and appreciative, and you said that you . . . uh . . ." She came to a puzzled stop. Could Irwin be in love with her? The idea had never occurred to her before. She'd always thought of him as a friend—her only friend, the one young man who'd never tried to impress her, the one who let her be herself. Was he going to ruin everything by acting like all the others?

Irwin's cheeks were pink. "Er, I was posing as one of your suitors, remember," he said. "But I'm glad I was so persuasive. Do you think I should go on the stage?"

Julia laughed, relieved. And yet . . . why didn't he love her? He knew her better than anybody else, and according to his song he admired her intelligence. Thinking back on the parts of the song she'd heard, she remembered that he hadn't mentioned her beauty. Did he think she was just a brainy drudge without any feminine charms? "Say, Irwin," she began, but she wasn't quite sure how to continue.

Just then they arrived at the coliseum, and Julia forgot about everything but negotiating the bleachers, taking their seats, and picking out Seymour's massive head among those of the other graduates. As trumpet blasts filled the air, Quentin the Hidebound strode to the podium to introduce the festivities. It was the most thrilling moment either Julia or Irwin had ever experienced, and even Richard looked impressed.

But after several hours of speeches and trumpet music under the hot sun, on the hard bleachers, Irwin's behind was sore, Julia steamed inside her golden kettle, Richard's feathers had wilted, and they all had headaches. Just as they were beginning to think longingly of home, confusion erupted on the field. A knight on a massive oil-black steed galloped across it and up onto the stage. He wore the latest silver armor and over it a pristine blue satin cloak with a red lining.

"Mortimer!" cried the crowd.

"Indeed, it is I!" replied the knight in a voice that rang across the land. He dismounted and handed his reins to his loyal steward, Vandeventer, who'd been so highly trained to fade into the background that nobody had noticed him until this moment, and everybody forgot him again at once.

With his back to the audience, Mortimer unbuckled his gauntlets and kicked off his boots. Off came his helmet, revealing a head of grizzled short hair. He unhinged his armor and stepped out of it. Finally, dressed in a simple tunic and socks, he turned to face the crowd, who stared at him in wordless astonishment.

Stripped of his fancy trimmings, Mortimer was an ordinary-looking middle-aged man with heavy jowls, crooked teeth, and a slight paunch. He scanned the coliseum through intelligent but not particularly steely eyes as a buzz of consternation slowly built. "*That's* the perfect hero, Mortimer?"

Mortimer smiled. "I take it you're surprised by my appearance." His voice, while pleasant enough, sounded nothing like the clarion call he'd issued moments before.

"No, no, not at all," replied the crowd unconvincingly.

"Oh, don't fib—I'm not what you expected. Admit it," said Mortimer. "You were imagining that I'd be six or seven feet tall, with sky-blue eyes and steel-colored hair that whipped in the wind. You thought I'd be craggy as a mountainside, leathery as a saddle, sinewy as a cheetah. You're disappointed by the reality, aren't you? Come on, don't be polite. Admit it."

"Well, a little," came a few voices. "Sure. Who could blame us?"

Mortimer nodded. "Why do you think I've never appeared in public before? It's because I knew that I was no match for my legend. But how, you may wonder, did the legend get started in the first place? How did *I*, a nice enough guy but nothing to write home about, ever get a reputation as the most dashing hero in the world?"

His question sounded rhetorical, so nobody broke the suspenseful pause that followed. Mortimer had just opened his mouth to answer it himself when he caught sight of a waving hand, way up in the bleachers. "Er, yes?" he asked in surprise. "Do you have any thoughts?"

Irwin had been waiting for this moment all his life. "You just focused on your work, doing good deeds and helping people, and although you never sought fame, it found *you*!" he shouted triumphantly.

The crowd sat perfectly silent with awestruck faces, as though they finally understood the true meaning of heroism. They looked even more surprised when Mortimer shouted, "You're absolutely wrong! Of course I did good deeds, especially at the beginning, but more important than doing them was spreading the word. Anybody can slay a dragon—they're peaceable creatures,

71

fond of blueberry pancakes—but you need a comprehensive program of advertising and public relations to stand out from the crowd. I'm not talking about a boast here or there. While my rivals were doggedly accomplishing feats, leaving the legend-building to bystanders, I took the time to come up with every detail of my own reputation and get it out there on the gossip circuit. Soon my name was enough to send the dragons running for their caves, and my feats more or less performed themselves." He surveyed the graduates with a knowing smirk. "Now, you boys may think you're so great that you don't need to advertise. But I've been out there, and I'm telling you it's a brutally competitive market. My program is the *only* way to make a living as a hero. Want to hear more?"

"Please, tell us more!" cried the students.

Mortimer held up a small leather book. "You've all probably been taught to record your exploits in a notebook. Well, I did it, and it served me well, but I got a bad case of tennis elbow from trying to gallop and write at the same time." He held up a second book with all sorts of peculiar attachments. "That's why I designed my own Heroic Feat Recording System, with a handgrip, hip rest, and shoulder strap. It's just one of many products in my new line of Mortimer Heroic Accessories, which I'm making available exclusively to Academy graduates for a limited time. You'll love how smoothly the patented Mortimer Quill Pen flows on the Mortimer Parchment, and if you buy both today, you'll also get a free copy of my invaluable book *How Big Was the Dragon? Mortimer's Guide to Memorable Exaggeration.*"

Up in the bleachers, Irwin's mouth opened wider and wider, until at last it could open no further and snapped shut by itself. Blinking, he turned to Julia, whose left eye, pressed to the buttonhole in her armor, was fixed on him. Even without the rest of her face it conveyed strong skepticism.

"I'm sorry," said Irwin, pale with shock. "This isn't what—you have to believe that I never imagined. . . ." Suddenly the situation struck him as so absurd that he giggled. "I fell for a con! Seymour used to tell me that Mortimer was in it for the money like everybody else, but I refused to believe it. All these years I've idolized him and compared everybody unfavorably to him. I've been so hard on poor Seymour, expecting him to live up to this ideal that didn't even exist. No wonder he got sick of me and my lectures!" His laughter subsided and he looked glumly at his feet. "What an idiot I've been."

Julia put her clumsy golden gauntlet on his shoulder. "Don't feel so bad. After all, you only wanted Seymour to be as great as you know he could be. Your expectations helped bring out his natural honor, decency, and pure-heartedness, and the world will be a better place for it."

Down on the stage, Mortimer had just finished modeling his heroic fashions. The graduates mobbed the stage, and Vandeventer efficiently collected their money.

Amid the fracas, Quentin took the podium again to invite the audience to a reception with ale and wild boar in the ballroom.

Irwin stood up. "I'm going to apologize to Seymour. Would you like to come?"

Julia hesitated. Her helmet had never fit right after it fell off that time, and if she lost it in a ballroom full of ambitious heroes, the results could be disastrous. But she couldn't resist a chance to talk to her hero again face to face—or face to buttonhole, at least. "Let's just try to be inconspicuous," she told Irwin as he guided the bonging armor down the narrow coliseum stairs.

Unfortunately, she'd picked the wrong outfit for the plan. Although the armor was old-fashioned, poorly cared for, and silly, it had obviously cost a great deal to make, and as soon as Quentin saw it, his eyes narrowed speculatively. A wealthy former hero could be prevailed upon to donate money to the Academy, which was having some financial problems. He waylaid Julia at the door and plied her with ale, boar shanks, and flattery. When Irwin tried to draw her away, Quentin cut him dead with a cold stare. "I believe there's a separate refreshment table out back for the stewards," he hissed. "Scraps and orts—every underling's favorite. Now run along. Shoo."

Helplessly, Irwin slumped off and waited for Julia at the ale dispenser. A heavy hand fell on his shoulder, brushed against Richard, and jerked away.

"Ugh," said Seymour. "Is this the same bird I rescued or a new one? Never could understand your fascination with the creatures. Well, Irwin, thanks for coming. What'd you think of Mortimer? Does he live up to your image?"

Irwin sighed. "Oh, Seymour—don't rub it in. You knew the truth all along, and I've been an idealistic dope. I'm glad to see that you didn't waste any money on his overpriced products."

Seymour shook his head. "Oh, no, I don't need to buy any of those."

"That's what we thought you'd say," said Irwin. He spotted Julia across the room shaking hands with the board of directors. "But come with me for a moment. You'll never believe who's here."

"After all, if I'm going to be selling them, I'll get all I need for free," continued Seymour.

"It's your old friend Sir—" Irwin cocked his head. "Selling what?"

"The Mortimer Line of Heroic Accessories!" said Seymour. "He invited me to work for him. I can make my fortune in a few years, he says, and by then things will probably have picked up in the quest business. As Mortimer pointed out, there's no use in wasting my talents on ant infestations. Until a real challenge comes along, I might as well save some money. Well, I'd love to catch up a little more, but I see Vandeventer waving to me. We've got a lot of stops on our first international sales junket, and we're setting off tonight. I'll send you a postcard!"

"Wait, Seymour!" cried Irwin.

But his old friend was already halfway across the room.

Irwin spent the rest of the afternoon following Quentin and the board of directors as they took Julia on a tour of the grounds, pointing out places where a generous supporter's name in solid gold letters might brighten up a facade. Finally they heard the dinner bell, and Julia was able to escape their clutches.

The experience had put her in a grouchy mood, and hearing about Seymour's new career made her even angrier. "What's happening to the world? Does anybody care about anything but money? However well Mortimer's paying Seymour, he's completely overqualified for the job."

Irwin shrugged. "But he's overqualified for everything else, too. The world is just not hard enough for somebody so extraordinary. If only a true challenge would come along, then he could achieve his full potential."

Julia stopped and turned to face him. Her eye, framed by the buttonhole, shone brightly. "What about a tournament?" she exclaimed. "An impossible, highly selective tournament for the hand of the most beautiful princess in the land!"

"Well, that would be great, but how do you know the princess would go for the idea?" asked Irwin. "She might be seeing somebody."

Julia's eye narrowed. "I'm talking about myself!" she snapped. "Really, Irwin, I know you don't think much of my looks, but it *is* widely said that I'm—"

"That's not what I meant," stammered Irwin in embarrassment. "It's just that I didn't know you were old enough to get married."

"I'll be fifteen in three days," sniffed Julia. "I've done some research into marital traditions, and if a true hero hasn't asked for a third princess's hand by her fifteenth birthday, her parents can hold a competition to find him. It will be expensive, but I can easily re-allocate money from the arms budget, and— Irwin? You're not saying anything. Are you afraid that Seymour won't want to give up his glamorous new career for a tournament?"

"Oh, no, I'm sure he will," said Irwin in a vague way. "If there's jousting involved, especially."

"Then what's wrong? You don't seem like yourself."

He didn't feel much like himself, either, he realized. "I'm just a little tired."

"Get some sleep, then," said Julia. "You'll need all your energy if you're going to make the caramels for my wedding next week!"

Irwin could barely smile. "Well, take good care of Richard for me—I mean, for Seymour. Richard, you know where to come if you want caramels." He patted Richard on the head, gave Julia a halfhearted wave, and staggered toward home.

"How odd," Julia said to Richard. "It's almost as though he's not happy for me." She glanced at the raven and jumped at the exasperated expression in his eyes. "Goodness, Richard. Have I done something to offend you?"

But Richard's eyes looked again like blank, bright beads.

"Of course. How thoughtless of me. You must miss Seymour most of all," said Julia. "But don't worry. I'll get him back for you. I'm going to talk to my parents right now."

Chapter 10

When Julia waded into the throne room, her parents were hard at it, as always.

"Oh, Virgil, here's a real moral dilemma," Queen Marianne was saying. "This fellow's wife is pregnant and craving lettuce that grows in a neighbor's garden. The neighbor is a witch, so he doesn't want to borrow any, but he doesn't feel right about stealing it, either. So here's what I have so far: 'Dear Fed Up with Her Cravings: Get over it. Climbing over a garden wall is nothing compared to having a baby.' Do you think that's too harsh? Oh, hello, darling," she said, looking up at her daughter.

"Guess what! I'll be fifteen on Monday," Julia announced.

Her parents looked at each other in surprise. "Goodness, already?" asked King Virgil. "I suppose a tournament is in order."

Queen Marianne frowned. "The true hero hasn't shown up? Are you sure? But what a silly question—you'd know it if he had. Oh, dear. I blame myself. Other kingdoms do a heavy publicity blitz for their fourteen-year-olds, but we never thought that would be necessary. I figured at least one of those heroes outside would be true." She sighed. "Things were simpler when we were young."

"Yes, your mother didn't have such high standards," joked King Virgil. "If she'd had hundreds of heroes to choose from, I doubt I would have impressed her, either."

"Silly goose!" cried the queen, swatting him lovingly with an envelope. "I'd have picked you from a thousand."

Julia removed a mailbag from her own throne and sat down in it. "Mom, how *did* you know you wanted to marry Daddy? Did you love him the moment you met him?"

"Since I was asleep at the time," said the queen, winking at her husband, "I'd have to say not. By the time I woke up, he'd already kissed me, and it wouldn't have looked right not to marry him after *that*."

"Fastest pucker in the west. Kiss first, explain later—
that was my motto," boasted the king.

"Then, Daddy, why did *you* fall in love with *her*?" Julia
asked him.

"Just look at her!" he said.

"But you didn't know how beautiful she was before
you hacked your way through the forbidding briars that

surrounded the kingdom where she lay in enchanted slumber," persisted Julia. "What made you try in the first place?"

"Well, I'd heard tell of her legendary beauty, of course, but to be honest, I wasn't planning to do more than look until I arrived. I knew that other princes had died trying to get in, and I wasn't an idiot. But there was just something about those briars. Trust your instincts—that's my best advice."

Julia sighed. "It's easy for you to say. Everything worked out for you. But even if we have this tournament, there's no guarantee that Seymour—er, I mean, the true hero—will even enter. Why couldn't *I* have been cursed by a fairy to fall asleep on my fifteenth birthday?"

"It's not as if we didn't try to arrange it," said her mother, a little irritably. "At *my* christening, my parents invited only twelve of the thirteen fairies in the kingdom, because they had only twelve golden plates for them to eat from. The thirteenth got mad and cursed me to prick my finger on a spindle—well, you know the story. So naturally we tried to repeat this tradition and left Wendy out, but she just assumed her invitation had been lost in the mail and showed up anyway. She didn't even object to eating off a silver plate!"

The king shook his head ruefully at the memory. "We waited all evening for somebody to lose her temper and curse you, but they all remained in fine spirits and heaped blessing after blessing upon you! Would you believe we considered planting briars around the kingdom ourselves? In the end we decided the upkeep would be too costly." He licked an envelope. "So I guess we'll have to scare up that hero with a really rigorous tournament. I'll make an announcement first thing tomorrow. But this occasion calls for something a little special. Marianne, do you happen to know where my armor is?"

"Maybe in the downstairs closet," said the queen. "But don't tell me you're going to wear that frightful old thing. I still remember those lapels!"

"Hey, I didn't hear any complaints back *then*!" said the king, tickling his wife, who shrieked with girlish giggles. "Especially under the moonlight—"

Everybody stopped laughing abruptly when a green young woman appeared in the doorway. She would have been very pretty, except that she wore a sour expression and lightning crackled from the ends of her magenta hair.

"Oh, hi, Murgatroyd-Liza!" said the queen with forced cheer, straightening her crown. "I didn't know you were coming home today."

"I'm just picking up some of my old things," said Murgatroyd-Liza. "Before *she* takes them all," she added, glaring at Julia.

"Nonsense, sweetheart," chided Queen Marianne. "Your sister has plenty of things of her own."

"Yes, because you give *her* whatever she wants," said Murgatroyd-Liza. "You're even holding a tournament for her, I couldn't help but overhear. It's not fair! She has all the heroes in the world at her beck and call. *I'm* the one who needs a tournament."

"Well, you should have thought of that before you chose a life of evil, sweetheart," argued her father.

"With a name like Murgatroyd-Liza, what other career was open to me?" she screeched. "You'll be sorry! I'm going to wind up with a better husband than *she* will, and I'll do it all myself. I have a malevolent plan, and—"

"Oh, that's wonderful, honey!" cried her mother. "I *knew* you could come up with one if you just had a little faith in yourself. I realize there's a lot of pressure on you—your sister Mimi is so wicked, and you've had to live in her shadow, but I just know that you, too, can—"

"Will you stop being so supportive all the time!" sobbed Murgatroyd-Liza. "I'm trying to *threaten* you! You're supposed to be *scared*!"

"I'm sorry, sweetie. I *am* scared, I promise, even if I don't always act that way," said Queen Marianne. "Now wipe your eyes and come see the new blood-red cape and cap I'm making you."

While Murgatroyd-Liza tried on her new clothes, Julia sneaked away to return Sir Bildungsroman to the downstairs closet. She closed the door on his familiar golden glow with a sinking heart. She hadn't had any specific plans for him, but she hadn't bargained on losing him. Now she'd definitely have to stay inside until the tournament was over, leaving her future in the hands of destiny.

Julia felt a prickle of worry. Could she trust destiny?

Chapter 11

The next morning, the king stood on the balcony in his armor and issued an invitation to all qualified princes and heroes to compete in history's most challenging tournament, which would start in two days. Only those who had inherited or made a large fortune would be permitted to enroll. The nature of the contest would not be revealed until enrollment had closed, but it was guaranteed to identify the true hero, whose reward would be Julia's hand in marriage.

Word quickly spread to the four corners of the earth. Irwin's parents could talk about nothing else at dinner that evening, picturing thousands of hungry heroes with broken hearts taking solace in caramel.

"What's wrong, dear?" asked his mother, Melinda. "You're awfully quiet."

"I feel a little odd," admitted Irwin.

"Gregor, get the manual!" shouted Melinda in terror. Her husband dropped his fork and scuttled out of the room.

"Oh, not the manual!" groaned Irwin, but Gregor was already staggering back in with their child-rearing guide, an enormous, dusty book that, despite its unpromising appearance, had always contained startlingly relevant answers to their most obscure questions. Irwin admired it far less than they did, having swallowed too many of its foul-tasting tonics over the years. He sulked at his dinner plate as they pored over the table of contents.

"Here," Gregor said triumphantly, poking a spot on the page. "Chapter 797: 'Unexplained Grouchiness After Announcement of Tournament for Princess's Hand.'"

"What?" asked Irwin, snapping to startled attention as they paged through the book. "It has nothing to do with *that*. It's just a low-grade fever."

"Yes, fever's one of the symptoms," Melinda said, ignoring him. She flipped another page. "Any dizziness?"

"Well, yes, now that you mention it," admitted Irwin. "But that doesn't—"

"Mm-hmm. And are you queasy at all?"

Irwin put both hands on his stomach. "Ugh. Yes. Maybe I had too many caramels today."

"Gregor, look in his eyes," Melinda told her husband. "Are they glassy with unshed tears?"

"Affirmative," said Gregor.

"His hands—trembling and cold?"

"Check."

"Knees—knocking?"

"Well, he's sitting down."

"They *were* knocking before!" cried Irwin, suddenly worried. "Mom, Dad? What's wrong with me? I have this strange sense of—"

"Overwhelming despair?" prompted Melinda. "As though a merciless hand is wringing your heart, your entrails are shriveling up and turning to ash, and your very bones are being riven and wrested from their sockets?"

"*Blecch*. Exactly," shuddered Irwin, feeling worse and worse.

Melinda looked up at Gregor. "That clinches it. He's lovesick."

Irwin sprang to his feet. "But that's outrageous! I've never been on a date. This time even *you* have to admit the manual doesn't know what it's talking about."

Gregor affectionately rubbed Irwin's head with his knuckles. "It's never failed us before, champ," he said. "Anyway, it only confirms what we've both suspected for years. You've got it bad, my boy. You're crazy about Julia! You think the sun rises and sets on—"

"Julia! But I . . . ," Irwin paused, all the air rushing out of his windy protests. "Well. I never would have admitted it, even to myself, but you're right. I do love Julia."

His parents nodded smugly at each other, patting the manual.

"I don't know what you're so cheerful about," added Irwin. "It's terrible news. I'm not worthy of her, and she'll marry Seymour or somebody better the day after tomorrow, and I'll have to spend the rest of my life heartbroken."

"According to the manual," said Melinda, squinting at the fine print, "there's only one cure for lovesickness: strong, decisive action toward achieving your heart's desire."

"You'll just have to enter that tournament and win her hand," concluded Gregor.

"Do you know unrealistic you're being? I'm not even qualified to enroll."

Gregor patted him on the back. "In my day, true love was the only requirement."

"Well, times have changed!" shouted Irwin, losing his temper. "You heard the announcement. I'm not a prince, and I'm certainly not a hero. No matter how much you love me, you can't deny the facts." His parents opened their mouths as though to protest, but then stopped when they realized that he was right. Irwin nodded. "And owning a candy shop that barely breaks even from month to month certainly won't count as having a fortune."

"What if we came up with a fantastic special—buy one, get one free?" said his father, brainstorming madly.

"Dad! Even the best special in history couldn't make me a fortune in two days! It's impossible!" Irwin pointed out. Seeing his father brighten, he added sharply, "And yes, some things *are* impossible."

His parents sat in silence for a while. Irwin felt bad for being so difficult. "I'm sorry. Would it be okay if I took a trip? Seeing Mortimer the other day gave me an idea. Everybody in Coriander loves our caramels, but nobody else has ever tried them. Maybe I could go to some neighboring kingdoms and drum up interest in a mail-order business."

"And make a fortune in the process!" his parents exclaimed in unison. "Brilliant! We'll rent you a mule and fill the saddlebags with caramels. Charge double or triple the price, and in no time you'll be rich enough to suit any princess. Do you suppose we should redecorate the shop in honor of the nuptials?"

Irwin clutched his head in exasperation while they rambled on and on, but he realized there was no point in arguing with them. They'd have to face reality soon enough.

Chapter 12

The next morning, Irwin set out into the wide world. He'd never taken a real trip before, and it should have been an exciting adventure, but he wasn't in any mood to appreciate it. His heart was so heavy that he didn't notice the beautiful golden fields or the brilliant blue sky. When he left the open country and entered the forest, he barely listened to the birds that trilled merrily in the rustling trees. As though hurt by his indifference, the landscape grew distinctly gloomier as he rode on. The trees got darker and more menacing, closing in on the narrow path and dangling spidery leaves in his face, and yellow eyes glowed at him from their branches. Just when he was becoming aware of how unpleasant things had become, the path ended altogether in a thick wall of cruel briars.

"I must have gone the wrong way," Irwin said in surprise. He tried to turn his mule around, but one of the briars had snagged his jerkin, working itself in so thoroughly that he couldn't free himself, and at last he had to take out his caramel knife and cut the branch.

At once the hedge burst into bloom, the briars turning into beautiful red and yellow flowers.

Irwin had heard enough news, and done enough of Seymour's homework, to have a sense of what was happening. There must be a kingdom inside the briar hedge, and a witch must have cast a spell on it. Some spells could be broken only by kisses, but most were scheduled to end after a preset period of time—one hundred years was standard. Obviously he'd happened by just as this one was coming full term.

"What a lucky coincidence," he said. "Everybody inside is probably waking up from a long sleep, and I'm sure they'll be hungry. Caramels to the rescue!" And he spurred on his mule.

After a brief gallop through a pleasant wood, he reached a public square very like the one in Coriander, except that there were no heroes in it, or anybody else—

only a number of bears hibernating on the cobblestones. They looked comfortable, even though they were fully dressed in clothes and hats. Had they always lived here? Had they moved in after the enchantment? Or had they once been people whom the witch had turned into bears? A quick look around suggested the last possibility: The cottages and shops were filled with bears, too, also dressed like people and looking as though they'd dropped off right in the middle of unbearlike activities, such as making supper, tanning leather, and playing cards.

"But if the enchantment has ended, why are they still bears, and why are they still sleeping?" he wondered.

He tied up his mule and pushed open the great doors to the castle. He marveled at the fine furnishings and the luxurious cloak the sleeping bear on the throne was wearing. Then he wandered into the back rooms, where the decor wasn't as nice and where bears in the clothing of servants dozed along with domestic animals. Finally, behind the kitchen, he came upon a wooden staircase that wound up a narrow tower to a shabby little attic. It contained nothing but a spinning wheel and a glass box lined in white velvet. The whole scene looked so much like the diagrams in Seymour's textbook that Irwin knew what he would find when he looked in the box, and sure enough, there was a beautiful princess.

She was dressed all in white and clutching a bouquet of lilies, and she lay motionless, her face as pale as her dress. The only signs that she lived were the faint bloom on her cheeks, the shallow rise and fall of her chest— and the way her eyes flew open and gave him a shrewd glance as he stared at her in wonderment.

Irwin jumped so high he bumped his head on the low ceiling. "I beg your pardon!" he exclaimed. "I thought you were asleep." Too late, he realized that this sounded even worse, as though he habitually crept into sleeping princess's bedrooms.

"Oh, I am!" said the princess, squeezing her eyes shut. "I'm deeply asleep. Sometimes, you know, you can be so asleep that you *seem* awake to others. Does that ever happen to you?"

"Er, well, no," admitted Irwin. But she looked at him again, this time so crossly that he added, "Of course I've never been enchanted, so . . ."

The princess nodded. "Exactly! It's a feature of enchanted slumber—seeming to be awake. But really I'm sleeping soundly. There's only one thing that would wake me up—and you and I both know what it is." She pouted her lips expectantly, and her eyelids fluttered shut. After a few minutes, when nothing happened, she opened them again. "Do I need to spell it out? I'm referring to a kiss from a true hero!"

"Well, I'm afraid I can't help you there," sighed Irwin. How disappointing to come all this way for nothing. "I thought the enchantment had been broken, but obviously I was wrong, so I won't disturb you." And he turned back toward the staircase.

The princess sat bolt upright. "Wait a minute! Aren't you going to kiss me?"

"*Me*?" asked Irwin, wheeling around. "Why would you want *me* to kiss you?"

The princess narrowed her eyes. "Why wouldn't I? I'm a princess, aren't I? I'm dressed like a princess, and I'm sleeping in a glass box in this filthy, bat-infested attic, so who else would I be? And what princess wouldn't want to be kissed awake by a true hero?"

"A true—!" Irwin's mouth hung open, and then he began laughing. "You really must be asleep if you think I'm a true hero. When you wake up you'll have a good chuckle about it." He turned to go.

The princess hopped out of the glass box and rushed around him to block the doorway. "Oh, no you don't.

Did or did not the briar hedge burst into bloom when you tried to hack your way through it?"

Irwin shrugged. "I wasn't exactly trying to hack my way through it, but, yes, it did flower when I cut it with my knife. A coincidence, obviously, since my knife has never had such a botanical effect before."

The princess folded her arms. "There's no such thing as a coincidence when you're dealing with magic. I—er—I mean, the witch who put the spell on this kingdom specifically programmed the hedge to keep out everybody but the true hero."

"Then I'm afraid it's malfunctioning," said Irwin. "I didn't even get into the Heroic Academy."

The princess reared back in dismay. "You *didn't*?" She bit one of her long blood-red fingernails—a discordant touch in her all-white outfit, which Irwin hadn't noticed before.

"I'm afraid not," he sighed. The old failure still stung. "So, if you'll let me past, I'll get out of your way—but don't worry. There are thousands of true heroes, and if you just put everything back the way it was, I'm sure one will come along soon."

"You mean go through all that again?" The princess seized his shoulders and pushed him back. "Come to think of it, people put too much stock in academic credentials in our society. If the hedge was okay with you, then I am, too. Now stop selling yourself short! This is a great opportunity. Not only do you get to marry *me*, but as if that weren't enough of an incentive, you'll inherit this kingdom, too—the Kingdom of Couscous, as it was known before the enchantment. Not bad, huh? All for one kiss. Power! Glory! Fame! Money! The envy of your friends and family!" And she flung her arms around his neck and brought her pursed lips right up to his face.

Irwin couldn't help being flattered. He'd always secretly thought he had the makings of a hero, but nobody had ever seemed to agree—until this princess and her briar hedge. If he won her hand and became king, everybody would have to acknowledge that they'd been wrong about him. The Academy would issue a public apology, and Seymour would come to him for advice. His parents would rename the shop Heroic Candies and make a fortune in their dotage. Julia would bitterly regret the opportunity she'd lost.

He closed his eyes and leaned closer. Right before his lips touched the princess's, though, he stopped. He didn't know anything about her, and he certainly didn't love her. It would be unfair to her, as well as to himself, to

kiss her when he really wanted to kiss somebody else. He sighed. "I can't do it, I'm afraid."

"Why not?" shrieked the princess, stamping her foot so hard that a flake of white powder fell off her cheek, exposing a patch of green skin beneath.

"Er," said Irwin uncomfortably, "your makeup. . . ."

"Grrrrr!" Now you've ruined everything!" The princess shook her head so hard the rest of the powder flew off, her golden hair turned magenta, and she rose in the air before him, suddenly wearing a blood-red cape, with lightning crackling from all her extremities. She raised her hands above her head menacingly.

"Hey!" cried Irwin. "You're not a princess at all! You're a wicked witch!"

Chapter 13

The witch's lower lip trembled. "There's no need for name-calling," she said. Her hands dropped to her sides, bright yellow tears oozed out of her eyes, and she crumpled into a colorful heap on the floor.

"I didn't mean—" said Irwin. "It's just a turn of phrase."

"Oh, I know," she sobbed. "And ordinarily I would take it as a compliment, but I'm just feeling a little vulnerable. I really believed you were the one."

"I'm sorry," said Irwin sincerely. He knew how

painful lovesickness could be, and although he found it very implausible, this witch really seemed to like him. "Please don't take it personally. It's not you; it's me. You came up with a very good plan to trap me, and if I'd just been in a different frame of mind—"

The witch looked up with tear-streaked cheeks. "Oh, you're just trying to make me feel better. I know you weren't fooled for a second."

"Sure I was! The woods were really creepy, and that briar hedge was perfect. I thought the bears were a nice variation on the theme, too. If I had to pinpoint the moment when I became suspicious, I guess it was when I noticed that your eyes were open. You recovered pretty well, but it's always hard to accept that a person who is having a conversation with you is asleep. Next time you might—" he paused as she lowered her head. "Is this criticism too harsh?"

"Not at all! It's great to get feedback from an intended victim's perspective," said the witch, glancing up from the notebook where she was furiously scribbling. "So that's what ruined everything? The open eyes?"

"Hmmm," said Irwin. "I don't know if even that would have stopped me from kissing you, if I hadn't already lost my heart to somebody else."

The witch sighed. "The best ones are always taken." She closed her notebook and got to her feet. "Well, I guess I'll have to reset the hedge and get back in that coffin. It's so boring in there, I couldn't help peeking, and who knows how long I'll have to wait? I don't suppose you have any single heroic friends you could send my way?"

"Actually I know quite a few heroes," said Irwin. "And I'd be happy to refer one to you, except—well, what would you do to him?"

The witch looked a little offended. "That's none of your business! I don't ask what you and your girlfriend do when you're alone."

Irwin sighed. "I mean, would you turn him into a toad or boil him in a cauldron or roast him in an oven?"

"Oh." The witch thought it over. "Maybe not every day, no, but often enough to keep the marriage healthy."

Irwin's jaw dropped. "Eh . . ."

"Kidding!" said the witch, slapping her knee and guffawing. "You should have seen your face! I really had you going, huh? No, I can turn people into frogs anytime, and I've never been much of a cook. Heck, I'd like to tell you I had something nasty up my sleeve, but the dull truth is, I'm tired of my wicked lifestyle, and I'm ready to settle down."

Irwin leaned against the spinning wheel. "Can I ask you a question, then, Ms. . . . ?"

"Murgatroyd-Liza," supplied the witch.

"Bless you," said Irwin, offering her a clean hanky.

"No, that's my name," she said grimly. "It's a doozy, isn't it? Can you blame me for turning out badly? 'Old family tradition,' my parents tell me. Ha! Anyway, what was your question?"

"Oh, right," said Irwin. "Well, if you're really interested in finding a husband, I was wondering if enchanting a kingdom is the best way to do it."

Murgatroyd-Liza chewed a fingernail pensively. "I guess it *would* be less tiring to enchant a village or hamlet, or maybe just a shop, but would such a small-time spell attract the best heroes? It could take me years to trap one that way."

Irwin sighed. "But what I mean is, there are other ways to meet people, even heroes, besides trapping them."

"No way!" snapped Murgatroyd-Liza. "I am *not* going on any more dates. It's always the same story. No matter how nice the guy seems, by the end of the evening he's a wild beast!"

Irwin coughed. "Do you mean," he said delicately, "that your dates get fresh with you, or—"

"No, I'm saying they actually turn into animals! An elephant on one occasion, a snow leopard another time, at least three flounders . . . or was one a minnow? Plus every sort of barnyard creature and enough birds to fill a sycamore forest."

Irwin was stumped. "That seems very odd. I can see that it might happen once or twice, but every time—it's a bit too much to be chalked up to accident."

"Oh, it was no accident," said Murgatroyd-Liza darkly. "Every last one of them had it coming. Claiming they needed time to 'think it over'! Suggesting they didn't like me 'that way' and wanted to be 'just friends'! Hah!"

Something dawned on Irwin. "*You* turned your dates into animals?"

Murgatroyd-Liza nodded smugly.

"That wasn't very nice, was it?"

Her hair crackled. "Well, what else was I supposed to do to them? It's the only spell I really know."

"But why did you have to do anything to them?"

"Duh!" sang the witch, mock-punching Irwin on the shoulder. "Because they didn't want to marry me!"

"But you didn't give them a chance!" said Irwin. "You can't propose to somebody on the first date and expect him to say yes. You have to get to know him first. Let him get to know you. Then you can think about building a life together."

Murgatroyd-Liza chewed another fingernail. "How long do you figure something like that would take?"

"Well, I can't really say. Some people are best friends after ten minutes, while others never understand each other."

Murgatroyd-Liza smiled coyly. "You and I seem to have hit it off pretty well, after our rocky beginning. You're certainly nicer than any of the other guys I've dated." She ran her fingernail down his cheek. "It almost seems a shame to turn you into an animal."

"Er," said Irwin.

"Kidding!" whispered Murgatroyd-Liza as her fingernail made its way to his neck. "But you know, I can't help wondering—if you're dating somebody else, then what are you doing here with me?"

Irwin sighed. "I didn't say I was dating her. I'm just in unrequited love with her."

"Well, the same question applies," cooed Murgatroyd-Liza, now running the fingernail into his collar. "You're not going to win her heart by gallivanting all over the countryside having flings with witches."

"I'm not—" Irwin gently removed her hand from his collar. "It doesn't matter what I do. She wants to marry somebody truly magnificent."

"More magnificent than you?" asked the witch.

Irwin blushed. "I'm really not magnificent. If you saw Seymour, you'd understand why I don't impress Julia."

"Julia!" cried the witch, rising in the air again in a snarl of lightning bolts. "I should have guessed!"

"Why—do you know her?"

"Not really, but I've certainly heard more than I ever wanted to about her," growled the witch as the lightning faded and she floated back down to the ground. "She's always been a spoiled brat, but this is ridiculous. If she has a guy like you after her, what does she need a tournament for?" She shook her head. "It's just her selfish scheme to get all the good ones for herself. How can you still care about her after she's treated you so shabbily? Is it her beauty?" She rolled her eyes.

"That's what first got me interested, sure, but as I got to know her, I found her intelligent and well-read and kind, and so good at doing dreary, daunting things—"

"All right, all right," snapped the witch. "Why don't you marry her, if you think she's so great?"

"I told you," said Irwin. "She doesn't want to marry me. I don't even qualify to enter her tournament. I'd have to be a prince or a hero, and I'm just a humble shopkeeper."

"But that briar hedge is pretty discerning, and *it* certainly thought you had the goods." Murgatroyd-Liza rubbed her chin. "It seems a shame that a few superficial details would keep you out. The crown prince of Couscous would have no trouble qualifying."

Irwin smiled wanly. "That's true."

"I'm serious!" said the witch. "I have a deal with the king. He has no heir, you see. Before I enchanted the kingdom, he signed this contract agreeing to adopt the young man of my choice." She took a folded piece of parchment from her cloak and held it out. "The enchantment will officially end only when a young man signs it."

Irwin studied it. "It says that if the young man doesn't marry you, you'll wreak merciless vengeance upon all Couscous."

"Hey, what are you, a lawyer, eagle eyes?" The witch took back the contract and scribbled out a sentence. "I wrote this before I met you. Obviously that part wouldn't apply. You can have the place with no obligation, my treat."

Irwin stared at her in amazement. "You'd do that for me? After I disappointed you?"

The witch waved her hand dismissively. "Oh, please. It was a youthful infatuation. We've both grown up a lot since then."

"But how will you trap a real hero, if you waste your evil scheme on me?"

The witch shrugged. "The evil scheme has a lot of problems. Even if a more gullible hero came along, it would be hard to persuade him to sign a contract, and anyway, I like your idea about getting to know somebody first. Now don't you worry about me. You're the one who needs a leg up right now." She handed him the contract and pen. "What are friends for?"

111

"Well, if you're sure." Irwin bent his head over the contract and wrote an *I* and an *R*. "I just can't thank you enough," he paused to say. "You know, I've always heard witches were unreasonable, and I guess I used to think of you that way when we first met, but I obviously underestimated you. You're a truly caring person. When you find your husband, he'll be a lucky man."

"I'm so glad to hear you say that," said the witch with a sanctimonious smile. "Now finish signing, dear, so you can meet your new daddy."

Irwin wrote the *W* and another *I*. Suddenly he remembered something. "Oh! I can't get adopted. I already have parents."

"So? The more the merrier. They won't mind, will they? It's not like they're losing a son—they're gaining a kingdom!"

Irwin thought this over. His parents would be so proud of him for becoming a crown prince that they surely wouldn't question his methods. He wrote the *N* and handed the contract back to Murgatroyd-Liza, who folded it carefully and put it in her cloak. "Let's go down to the throne room. The curse is ended, and the king should be awake."

Chapter 14

Irwin and Murgatroyd-Liza made their way down the rickety old staircase and through the back rooms of the castle. No longer bears, the servants were standing up, finishing the sentences they'd been halfway through when they fell asleep, and stoking fires and milking cows as if nothing had happened. In the front hall, courtiers were staggering to their feet and resuming their arch banter, and a fine-looking old gentleman had replaced the bear in the throne. Perhaps because of his advanced age, he seemed to be having a harder time waking than the others, and he blinked groggily as the witch led Irwin up to him.

"Well, Kingy," said Murgatroyd-Liza, slapping him on the back. "Last time we spoke I said you wouldn't wake up until you had a son. So, here's your bouncing baby boy—all grown up!"

Irwin felt shy. "Er, nice to meet you," he said. "I hope you don't think . . . er . . . I mean, this probably seems a bit pushy of me, but I will endeavor to deserve . . ." He paused, wishing he were better at introductions. "Do you like sports?" he asked awkwardly after a moment.

The king's eyes fluttered closed, and he dropped his chin to his chest and snored once before jerking awake and looking around in fresh bewilderment.

"How I wish I'd brought my oil paints," said Murgatroyd-Liza, watching with clasped hands, "to capture this touching first encounter between father and son. Now, you two get acquainted, have some laughs, and I'll be back tomorrow with a wedding dress and a five-piece orchestra. Toodle-oo!" She kissed Irwin lightly on the cheek and headed for the door.

Irwin was still trying to think of a way ingratiate himself with the bleary-eyed king. "Okay, see you . . . ," he called to Murgatroyd-Liza. "Wait a minute!" He turned to stare at her.

"Yes?" she called impatiently.

"Did you say something about a wedding dress?"

"Well, of course. You already saw me in my other one, and isn't that supposed to be bad luck? My older sister, Mimi, has this fabulous book of wedding spells."

"But—" gasped Irwin.

"Honey, I have a lot to do," said Murgatroyd-Liza. "Enchant a caterer, summon the demonic musicians, stop by my parents' place and tell them the good news. I'm not asking you to do anything but enjoy the last moments of your single life. But remember: no bachelor party! I'll see you tomorrow at the altar!"

"Altar," said Irwin slowly. "But we're not . . . we . . . you and I?"

The witch smiled indulgently. "Honey, every groom gets jitters." She unfolded the contract. "But you don't want me to wreak my fearsome vengeance on all Couscous, do you?"

Irwin looked in horror at the king, who, seeming to perk up at the suggestion, shook his head emphatically. Then he looked back at the witch. "But you scribbled that clause out!"

"Actually I just pretended to," said Murgatroyd-Liza, suppressing pleased giggles. "It's against the law to tamper with a contract, and I didn't want to risk making this one invalid."

There was a long pause. "Ha ha ha? You really had me going?" Irwin tried.

"Oh, dear," said Murgatroyd-Liza. "Your sense of humor is not your strong suit, I guess. I'm funny enough for two, so leave the joking to me, okay? You just focus on being cute, rich, and titled, and I'll see you tomorrow!"

And, in a puff of smoke, she was gone.

Irwin stared at the place where she had been.

The king, meanwhile, was slapping himself lightly on

the cheeks to restore circulation. "There's nothing quite like an enchanted slumber," he said, yawning. "All right, folks," he called regretfully to his courtiers. "Curse is lifted. Back to business."

The courtiers gave the room a quick sweep, set up card tables, and sat down to play bridge. The king put on a pair of spectacles and began reviewing unpublished edicts.

Irwin watched, taken aback by the court's nonchalance. "Have you been enchanted before?" he asked.

"Hmmm? Oh, yes, dozens of times," the king replied, looking over his spectacles. "I'm King Pignoli, by the way—you can call me Dad. I'll just call you Son—I'm too old to remember all these newfangled names. Yes, as I was saying, we used to spend about half our time asleep. We're the closest kingdom to the Witchy Woods, you see, and witches used to show up about once a week, make impossible demands, and put us to sleep until a hero came along. Then there was a long dry spell, when the heroes had beaten them back into the deepest forests, and I suffered insomnia for the first time in my life. But it seems as though they're up to their old tricks again." He smiled in satisfaction. "If the trend continues, you'll have a comfy rule—so long as you don't provoke their fearsome vengeance. *That's* when things get too hot to handle."

Irwin nodded glumly. "I was hoping the fearsome vengeance wasn't so bad."

"Oh, it's bad, all right," said the king with a shudder. "It must be, since nobody knows what it is."

"Then I guess the only responsible thing for me to do is to stay and marry Murgatroyd-Liza," sighed Irwin, "even though it means I must give up my own dreams."

"How true!" cried the king gratefully. "You're seeming more and more like the son I never had. I suppose I'll call off the army, then." He snapped his fingers, then paused and shot Irwin a keen glance. "On the other hand, one can never be too careful. You wouldn't mind staying in the tower, just until the wedding?"

"Oh. All right," said Irwin glumly, as a troop of four hundred shackled him and led him away.

Chapter 15

Julia's day had been much less exciting than Irwin's. In fact she'd never been so bored. She lay on her bed staring at the ceiling. There were hours left before tomorrow and no way to fill them. Tomorrow she'd find out whether Seymour had come. Tomorrow she'd learn if he was to be her husband. Tomorrow her life would change forever. But today there was nothing to do.

Everybody else in the kingdom was busier than ever preparing for the tournament. Even the wise men had gone off to criticize the design of the new coliseum, so council meetings had been suspended until after her wedding. At least, she told herself, it would all be over soon. Everything would work out for the best, as it always did in the news. Seymour would win the competition, they'd be married, and in a few days she'd be swamped with the work that was probably piling up in the council chamber.

Suddenly she sat up with a gasp. Wouldn't her husband, who by law would inherit the kingdom, run the council from now on? She'd meant to change those inheritance laws, but she'd never gotten around to it, and lovesickness had driven it right out of her head. What had she been thinking? She had no idea of Seymour's views on leadership, but here she was, scheming to deliver her populace into his hands. What if he turned out to be a cruel tyrant?

Julia shook her head and took a deep breath. Nobody with a brow as craggy as Seymour's could be anything but noble. She still remembered the look on his face the first time she'd seen him—how concerned he'd been about the survival of a complete stranger. Of course, as she'd found out later, he was being graded on it. But still, it was obvious that his heart was in the right place. They'd discussed politics as they sat in the woods together. At least, she'd talked to Irwin, and Seymour certainly hadn't disagreed. It had always been hard to tell if Seymour was even listening as he twirled, pranced, and strutted among the trees.

After all the hours she'd watched and admired him, she had no idea if he had the attention span to run a kingdom. It wasn't always glamorous or rewarding work. Sometimes Julia struggled for months to push through some tiny advance for the serfs, and the next time she saw them, they wouldn't seem much happier. What if Seymour got bored and left the dull, thankless parts to the wise men, while he reveled in the pomp and circumstance? What would happen to her fragile, enlightened state?

She heard a caw and turned to see Richard on his perch, staring at her with his beady eyes. She gulped in relief. "Richard!" she cried. "Richard, thank you for reminding me. You're living proof of Seymour's diligence. He stuck with you for years—until he got that ridiculous job, of course. No matter what he was doing at school, he always made the time to feed and care for you."

Richard rolled his eyes. "Silly," he said, in a hoarse but distinct voice.

Julia nodded. "It *was* silly of me to doubt him. It must have been nerves. If he wins tomorrow, I'll never—" She blinked and did a double take. "Richard! You can talk! Why have you concealed this talent all these years? Tell me about Seymour! You know him better than anybody else. Speak to me of his wisdom and nobility and greatness!"

Richard stared at her, his head cocked, his black eyes bright but impossible to read.

"All right, maybe you can't talk," conceded Julia. "But what you said sounded like a word, and that means you *could* talk if you were taught properly. I have the whole day free, and I'm not going to give up until you're speaking in full sentences. We'll start with a word close to your heart. I'll get the birdseed." She held some out to him on her palm. "Now, Richard, say *birdseed*."

Richard looked from her hand to her face.

"Bird. Seed. Bird. Seed. Bird. Seed. Birdseed," said Julia, enunciating each syllable.

Richard gave a tiny squawk.

"Very promising start!" said Julia. "You'll be chatting away in no time. Now, listen. Birdseed. Birdseed. Birdseed."

She paused for breath, wondering exactly how long it took to teach a bird to talk. Of course she had hours to spare, and it would show a distinct lack of fortitude to give up so soon. "Birdseed," she resumed. "Bird. Seed. Bird. Seed. Bird."

"All right, already!" Richard burst out in a furious screech. "Nobody's denying that it's birdseed. Revolting stuff. What's your point?"

Julia dropped the seeds and clapped both hands over her mouth. Richard stared back defiantly. "Well?" he asked after a moment, his tail twitching with indignation.

"So you *can* talk!" Julia exclaimed. "Why didn't you say anything when I asked you, instead of letting me go on and on about birdseed?"

"If you'll recall, you gave me very specific instructions about what to say," Richard replied haughtily. "And you can't blame me for not wanting to rush into a conversation with you. You obviously have a *very* particular way

125

of going about it. *Birdseed,*" he repeated, half under his breath, shaking his head.

He looked so cute that Julia wanted to pick him up and smooth his ruffled feathers, but she thought it might wound his dignity. "I see," she said humbly instead. "Well. Let's start over. How is it you can talk?"

"Evidently you believed you were the only one who could?" Richard demanded, hopping in agitation.

"No, of course not. But I don't know many talking birds."

Richard's hopping slowed. "It's true," he said regretfully. "Most of us aren't very bright. That's the only drawback to being a bird, I've found—you want for intelligent conversation. Although it doesn't take much to remind me"—he glared at the princess with renewed irritation—"that I didn't always get that from *people,* either. Birdseed!"

"Ah hah! I get it!" crowed Julia. "You weren't always a bird, were you? You used to be a prince, right? And an enchantment was put on you, and only true love can restore you to your human form?"

"Okay, first of all—" began Richard, rolling his eyes.

"Don't be shy. I'd be delighted to help!" exclaimed Julia. She paced around the room, squinting with concentration and biting her thumb. "I would have helped you years ago if you'd only told me. It's a little tricky, since I'm already in love with Seymour, but I don't think it would be disloyal to love you, too, under the circumstances. Now, how should I go about it? Love at first sight would be the most efficient strategy, but although I *liked* you right away . . . don't be hurt. You have to admit it would be strange. But now I know the truth— Please stop flying around in circles! Just sit still and let me work up some romantic thoughts." She looked around. "Richard? Where did you go?"

There was no sign of him. "Richard?"

"I'm in the chimney," came an offended squawk. "And I'm not coming out until you promise not to fall in love with me."

Chapter 16

Puzzled, Julia glanced in the mirror, where she saw the same exquisite portrait that had always greeted her there. "Is it my hair?" she asked at last, dubiously.

"No, of course not. Don't be absurd," screeched Richard. "Your hair is perfect. It's—wait a minute. Are you blushing and preening?"

"What? No!" said Julia unconvincingly, turning away from the mirror.

"You were!" said Richard. "Stop it! I'm not saying anything else until you promise to cease and desist all lovey-dovey behavior at once and forever."

"Fine. I promise," said Julia, crossing her arms. "I was

just trying to help. I knew all along there was no real future for us."

Richard's little black head poked out of the fireplace. He shook out his wings, sending up a cloud of soot. "Do I still look like a bird?" he whispered.

"More than ever," said Julia. "Now, what's going on here, Richard?"

He flew to the mirror and examined his reflection from all angles. "What a close call," he said. "I don't actually know if love *would* end the enchantment. But why take chances? I'm sorry I was so firm with you, but you could have ruined everything."

Julia watched him, baffled. "Are you saying that you don't *want* to be a prince again?"

"In the first place, as I was trying to tell you before you got so carried away—" He shivered at the memory. "I wasn't a prince. I only *worked* for one, as his valet. It was a terrific job—good pay, perks, two weeks' vacation. He was a fair master. My family was proud, and my friends envied me. But I had no passion for the work. I struggled to reconcile myself to my destiny, but I grew more and more depressed."

"So what happened?"

Richard hopped. "Unexpected fortune involving a relative of yours, coincidentally. Your sister Murgatroyd-Liza came by my master's castle one day looking for a husband. I said he'd be back in three-quarters of an hour. She said she couldn't wait but would *I* be interested in marrying her? I said no, thank you, and heard a funny little *ping*. Wondering what had made it, I hopped nimbly onto the table, then up into the rafters, and it was only when I felt a tickly sensation that I realized I was flying."

"Murgatroyd-Liza knows how to turn people into ravens?" said Julia. "That surprises me. My parents have given me the impression that she's not very good at her work."

"Oh, she's terrible!" agreed Richard. "She's famous in the forest for leaving behind human traits in her victims. Haven't you ever wondered why so many pigs walk on their hind legs and wear little waistcoats? Why monkeys often juggle? Why newts sing opera and toads give tax advice? Why I, a raven, can speak so eloquently in your native tongue? No wild creature would do anything of the sort if it weren't for Murgatroyd-Liza. I have no cause to complain, though. I love being a raven. I set my own schedule and answer to nobody, and since my adoption, I haven't even had to hunt for food. I've kept my ability to talk a secret for fear that somebody would fall in love with me or sell me to the circus. But that birdseed thing really pushed me over the edge."

"Then I'm the only one who knows the truth," said Julia.

"Er, well, not exactly," said Richard. "Irwin's known almost from the beginning."

"Irwin?" asked Julia in surprise.

"Sure. You know what a pleasant conversationalist he is—and what a good listener," said Richard. "And I knew he would never betray me."

Julia frowned. "I agree with you, and I suppose I understand why you didn't confide in me, but I still don't see why you kept it from Seymour. You owe him your life, after all. In all those weeks you've spent with him, you were really never tempted to thank him?"

Richard stared at her, then passed a wing over his eyes. "For an intelligent girl, you're very foolish," he said. "Irwin has been taking care of me all this time. I've never spent a moment with Seymour, and I'll be just as happy if I never see him again. He hates birds."

Julia blanched. "Hates birds? That's very— Well, but that makes his rescue of you even nobler."

Richard shook his head. "You didn't see what really happened that day at the riverbank. *Irwin* was the one who rescued both of us. Seymour just walked up and took the credit."

"That's ridiculous," said Julia. "I was there. I saw it." Hadn't she? She rubbed her eyes, trying to remember. "Anyway, if it is true, how come nobody's ever mentioned this to me before? Why didn't Seymour deny it? And how come Irwin has never told me the truth?"

"Simple. Seymour likes to be the center of attention, and Irwin doesn't. He's modest."

Julia frowned. "There's such a thing as being *too* modest. Maybe Seymour lied to me, but Irwin did, too."

"He just didn't want you to be disappointed," said Richard. "He could tell that you wanted to think highly of Seymour, and he hoped that Seymour would grow to deserve your admiration."

Julia folded her arms. "I don't care what his reasons were. He should have told me the truth."

Richard stamped his claw. "Would you have believed

him? Even now you refuse to admit that Irwin loves you, whereas Seymour doesn't love anybody but himself."

"Nonsense," said Julia. "Seymour just doesn't realize that he loves me. And Irwin thinks of me as a friend. He told me so."

Richard opened his beak, but just then Queen Marianne poked her head in the door. "Julia, I have a little treat for you," she sang.

"What is it?" asked Julia cautiously. A few moments earlier she would have hoped to hear that a craggy hero named Seymour had been seen in town, but suddenly she was too confused to know what she wanted.

The queen held out her arm. "Your sisters are here, and they have something to say to you."

Alarmed at the prospect, Richard flew into the chimney again.

"I hope your tournament goes well," said Mimi sourly, slinking into the room. She was eight feet tall and dressed so stylishly that everybody else suddenly felt shabby.

"Yeah, good luck finding your true hero," spat Murgatroyd-Liza with a malicious smile.

"Mimi and M.-L. are staying to supper!" cried the queen. "Won't that be lovely? The whole family together again at last. And Murgatroyd-Liza says she has a big announcement to make, too. Now let's all go down together before the soup gets cold."

In the dining room, they took their places at the long table, where an awkward silence prevailed. Julia, who usually tried to keep up a pleasant conversation at family gatherings, was too bewildered by Richard's disclosures to say anything.

"So, Julia," said Murgatroyd-Liza as the soup bowls were collected. "I ran into an old friend of yours the other day."

"Oh?" asked Julia politely, thinking it couldn't have been a very good friend.

"Yes. A wonderful young man. Good-looking, honorable—maybe a little short on wit but otherwise absolutely ideal. The one guy I've ever met who really qualifies as a true hero."

Julia paled. The description and Murgatroyd-Liza's dreamy tone were unmistakable. She had to be talking about Seymour! "How did *you* meet him?" she asked.

Murgatroyd-Liza shrugged airily. "He was looking for a princess to rescue, and let's just say I was in the right place at the right time."

Julia put down her soupspoon. "Looking for a princess? But isn't he on his way to enter my tournament?"

"Oh, he said he'd considered it but he'd never thought you really liked him that way. Luckily for him, not everybody is as disdainful as you." Murgatroyd-Liza blushed an attractive hunter green. "Mom, Dad, he's the man I've been looking for. We're getting hitched tomorrow."

She couldn't have wished for a more gratifying response. Everybody gathered around to praise and congratulate her—except Julia, who hung back with a stunned expression. Seymour thought she didn't like him? Then her mother's advice had backfired! All those years she'd been playing hard to get, she must have given him the impression that she didn't care at all. And now he was engaged to Murgatroyd-Liza. She'd set up a tournament to attract a man who didn't really exist—a man who wouldn't enter it even if he did. Now, because of her carelessness, a complete stranger would get to rule her kingdom. "Er, Daddy," she said hastily, "maybe there's no need to hold a tournament after all."

"Ha! I knew it!" crowed Murgatroyd-Liza. "Now that I've stolen away her true hero, she doesn't want to play anymore. Typical of Julia."

"Now, now," said Queen Marianne gently. "There are plenty of heroes to go around. I'm sure your sister's just thinking about timing. If we're all at the tournament, how can we attend your wedding tomorrow? Maybe we *should* reschedule, dear," she said to King Virgil.

"Er," said Murgatroyd-Liza. She hadn't planned on inviting her family to the ceremony. Irwin might make a break for the door, or sob and pray for mercy, and it would be safer to introduce them to him once the deed was done.

She smiled with relief when the king shook his head. "Can't reschedule now," he said. "But it will be my honor to announce M.-L.'s marriage at the same time I declare the victor of the tournament. Two daughters accounted for in one day! You sure you don't want to join the fun, Mimi? There will be plenty of heroes out there for the asking."

"Actually I've been in a long-distance relationship for many years, but my career's going so well I can't think about settling down now," said Mimi haughtily.

"Show-off," muttered Murgatroyd-Liza. "My career's going well, too, for your information. *I* just happen to be able to balance work *and* a social life."

"Girls!" said Queen Marianne. "This is a *happy* occasion."

"It sure is. I'd better give that armor an extra polish." King Virgil strode toward the door determinedly.

"Oh, no," sighed his wife and daughters in uncharacteristic harmony.

"What?" The king turned to look at them in surprise.

"It's just that, well, that armor is . . . ," said Queen Marianne, trying to be tactful.

"Totally uncool, Dad," put in Murgatroyd-Liza.

"Really square," added Mimi.

The king looked devastated. "Julia, do you agree with them?"

Julia was torn. She didn't want to hurt her father's feelings, but she liked the idea that Sir Bildungsroman would be free the next day. "You're so handsome, Daddy—why would you hide all that manly vigor behind a suit of armor?"

King Virgil drew back his shoulders proudly, and Queen Marianne cast Julia a grateful look. But Julia was thinking too hard to notice.

Chapter 17

The next morning, Irwin watched the sun rise from the Couscous tower. His room, at the very top, had been designed to imprison the most discriminating princesses, so it boasted all the modern amenities and was filled with devices for whiling away the years in ladylike ways: a spinning wheel with plenty of straw, a talkative mirror, and books of plaintive melodies to warble out the window. But Irwin didn't have a heart for these pursuits or an appetite for the freshly baked whole-grain bread and sparkling spring water he found on the sideboard. In a few hours he'd be married—to Murgatroyd-Liza, of all people.

It could be worse, he supposed. Yes, his fiancée was a witch—deceitful, inconsiderate, and tactless—but she was smart, too, with an offbeat sense of humor that he might, in time, come to appreciate. Maybe they'd grow truly fond of each other over the years, through the inevitable struggles— Oh, who was he kidding? Irwin had spent much of his life talking himself out of disappointment, but this time he just couldn't do it. He'd never love Murgatroyd-Liza the way he loved Julia.

How excited he'd been about entering the tournament! Of course he wouldn't have won—not against all those heroes—but at least Julia would have known how he felt about her. It seemed important that she know, even if it didn't change anything. But now it was too late. They'd both soon be married to other people, and it would be dishonorable to pine after her. He'd have to cram a lifetime of pining into his last few hours as a bachelor.

Just as he was getting into pining position, he heard a key in the door, and twelve of the wisest-looking men he'd ever seen filed into the room.

They all wore long white beards, long black robes, and small round spectacles, and they carried briefcases bulging with papers with complicated formulas scrawled all over them in tiny handwriting. Irwin shrank apologetically into the corner. His eyes and chin felt very bare, and he was suddenly ashamed of his tan jerkin—had it always been so gaudy and short?

"I am Eadric the Intellectual," said the first, bowing his head slightly, "and this is the council of wise men of Couscous. The king has informed us that you are his heir, and we have come to instruct you in matters of state. It is a great responsibility to rule a kingdom, young man—but of course you've entered into it with the proper solemnity."

Eadric's tone was skeptical, and Irwin remembered how casually he'd signed the contract. "I, er . . . ," he said. "I'll . . . I mean, I'll do my best . . . ah . . . not knowing very much about tax law, or economics, or foreign policy. . . . But I'm sure that good intentions will take me, you know, pretty far. . . ."

Eadric's eyebrows went up with every word, until at last they stopped just beneath his hairline. "I see we have our work cut out for us. Archibald, take notes," he said to the wise man to his left, who pulled out a small notebook. "He'll need intensive coaching in glibness. Meanwhile, cloak." He put out his hand, and Archibald draped an ermine cloak over it.

Eadric put the cloak on Irwin, who slumped under its weight, feeling even sillier than before. "Now walk," said Eadric.

Irwin took a few shuffling steps.

The wise men gasped in unison. "Oh, dear," said Eadric. "The populace will laugh you off the stage at the coronation ceremony. Shoulders back! Nose up!"

Irwin stopped short. The whole situation seemed painfully familiar. "Do you mean to say that being a prince is all about a special walk?"

"Certainly not *all* about it," said Eadric. "But you obviously bring very little to the role, and it never hurts to make a good first impression. The populace does enjoy a nice royal stride. Now just put that nose up and—"

Irwin threw off the cloak. "I'm sorry!" he cried. "I promised myself a long time ago that I would never again try to impress people by acting like somebody I'm not. My populace is just going to have to take me as I am: a simple, shy, socially awkward fellow who eats more caramels than he should and never knows the right thing to say. If they give me a chance, they'll find that I have a good heart. Otherwise they can revolt, for all I care. Now please let me pine in peace."

Grumbling among themselves, the wise men filed out. "I'm sorry you've decided to be so uncooperative," warned Eadric as he went. "We can be extremely condescending when crossed."

Irwin shuddered, but he decided there would be plenty of time to make amends once his doom was sealed. He turned back to the window to resume pining—only to find himself face-to-face with Seymour, who was climbing through it.

The two old friends stared at each other. "What are *you* doing here?" they asked at the same moment.

"It's a long story," Irwin answered.

"Mine, too," said Seymour. "That Mortimer thing didn't turn out the way I'd expected. He'd promised me a lot of responsibility, but do you know what he wanted me to do? Act in a ridiculous play. Vandeventer would pretend to buy Mortimer's products and then go off-stage. I was supposed to gallop heroically on, wearing the same clothes, as though the products had transformed him into me. Well, I quit on the spot."

Irwin nodded. "I'm glad. It's not nice to fool people."

Seymour snorted. "Not if you're going to do it so badly. Nobody would ever have believed that *I* was once a steward. I'd rather make my living as a hero, even if the pickings are slim. I heard that this place was enchanted, but when I got here I saw that somebody had already tripped the briar hedge, so I came in anyway to see if there are any remaining wrongs to be righted. Maybe even a spare princess to rescue."

Irwin stared at him. "But then you must not have heard. The tournament for Julia's hand starts today! There's still time to make it to Coriander before enrollment closes, if you ride like the wind."

"Oh," said Seymour uncomfortably, not meeting Irwin's eyes. "Actually, I have heard about it—it's the talk of the world, after all. And I'd love to enroll, honestly, but I'm just not sure I have the time today."

Irwin was baffled. Seymour had been complaining for years about the lack of real challenges in the world. Now that one had come along, why was he refusing to compete? Could he possibly be afraid he wouldn't live up to his own image? "Seymour, you're destined to win this tournament. You've spent your whole life training for it. There'll be hundreds of the world's finest heroes to beat, a coliseum filled with admirers to cheer you on, and a contest that will prove to everybody that you, and you alone, are a true hero!"

"Yes, yes, you have a point there," said Seymour, his eyes glowing as he stared off into space.

"Anyway, why would you want to rescue some strange princess from a tower you happened to pass, when you could win the hand of Julia, your childhood friend? I remember your once saying there were other princesses in the world. There may be a few as lovely and sweet as Julia, but I'm sure there are none with her seriousness of purpose, her enlightened politics, and the rare determination that enables her to go through piles of tedious paperwork that have bored others senseless. How I envy you!"

As he heaved a gusty sigh, though, he noticed that the gleam had gone out of Seymour's eyes. "Seymour?" he asked. "Do you still feel guilty about the way you treated her when we were kids? Because if that's the problem, she's long since forgiven you."

Seymour gave him a searching look. "Irwin, I have to level with you. I know you think Julia's the greatest, but to me she's always seemed, well . . ."

"What?" demanded Irwin, outraged.

"You always get so touchy about this subject," protested Seymour.

"I'm just very interested in what fault you could possibly find in Julia," said Irwin coldly.

Seymour sighed. "It's not so much a fault as—well, a lack of faults, really. She's so perfect, so full of wisdom and insight, courage and grace, so committed to the betterment of society. I can see what you're thinking: Who would complain about these qualities? And I have nothing but the greatest respect for her. But you know how I have a tendency to take myself too seriously. I need a girlfriend who shows me the silly side of life."

"Oh, if that's your only concern—Julia's just as silly as anybody else," said Irwin.

Seymour didn't look convinced. "Examples?"

"Why, there are hundreds of examples!" said Irwin. "So many that it's hard to pick one. Let me see. Oh! There was one time we were talking about labor unions and—no, that ended up on a serious note. Then there was that whimsical discussion of human rights, but I think you kind of had to be there. Huh. It's a strange thing, but I can't really think of any examples. But she's so delightful, the air around her is filled with happy laughter, and she doesn't need to tell jokes."

Seymour studied him for a moment. "Irwin, I may be self-absorbed, but even I've noticed that *you* seem awfully fond of Julia. Every boy at the Academy believed himself in love with her, but none of them matched you in devotion."

Irwin suddenly felt so lovesick that he had to sit down. "You're telling me. Why do the songs and poems make it sound *fun* to be in love?"

"I think a mild dose of it *can* be fun," said Seymour, feeling Irwin's forehead, "but I've never seen a case like yours. Winning Julia's hand would cure you. Too bad you don't even qualify for the tournament."

Irwin rubbed his swollen glands. "Oddly enough, I've become crown prince of this kingdom. But even if I enrolled, there's no way I could win."

Seymour gave him a reproving stare. "Certainly not—unless you try! You read my Tournaments textbook more closely than I did, and even I remember that true love always prevails, especially when it seems impossible. Don't let your fears stop you."

Irwin sighed even more heavily. "It's not just my fears. I'm already engaged. One of the conditions of my inheritance is that I marry a witch."

Seymour made a sympathetic face. "Yuck. A warty old hag? Well, don't judge her too hastily. Sometimes they're just enchanted. Maybe she'll surprise you and end up pretty."

"She's already pretty. But she might as well be a warty old hag as far as I'm concerned, for I can love only Julia. I told the witch so from the start, but she tricked me, and now I'm locked up in here until she comes back to marry me."

"What? You're here against your will?" cried Seymour, his chest puffing up and his golden-red curls tightening. "Why didn't you say so? I shall rescue you! To be honest, you could climb down yourself—it's not that tall a tower—but I'd appreciate the business. What do you say? For old times' sake?"

Irwin shook his head. "Thanks, but if I don't marry this witch when she returns in a little while, she'll wreak her fearsome vengeance on the populace of Couscous. It wouldn't be honorable to run out on them."

Seymour looked crestfallen. "Well, there's different ways of looking at it," he said. "I mean, it's not really *your* fault that—wait! Do you mean to say *everybody here* is a captive?"

"Well, yes, in a way."

Seymour's eyes looked flintier than ever. "Then I can rescue the lot of you! When the witch comes back, there'll be nobody here to wreak vengeance on. We can find you an equally nice kingdom somewhere else. Let's go explain the situation to the king. I did a project on large-scale rescues my senior year, so I can get everybody packed up and on the road in twenty minutes." He got out his Mortimer Heroic Feat Recording System—a gift from his old boss—and licked the tip of his pen. "Do you happen to have a recent population count? So many rescues in one day will make me famous worldwide."

Irwin bit his lip. "Oh, Seymour, I don't know. It seems like a lot of trouble, relocating an entire kingdom just so I can enter a tournament I can't win. And this witch is nobody's fool. What if she figures out where we've gone and comes after us?"

"You just let me handle her," said Seymour, busy recording his latest accomplishments. "I didn't take two semesters of Witch Wrangling for nothing, you know."

Chapter 18

Julia and Richard had stayed up all night trying to think of a plan that would get her out of marrying the winner of the tournament, but every idea had some fatal flaw.

As the sun rose, Richard shrugged his wings. "There's just no way out. I certainly hope you've learned your lesson, young lady. This all comes of trying to force destiny to bend to your will. You rigged this thing so that the wrong person would win—and so that the right person wouldn't even qualify—and now destiny's punishing you for your arrogance."

"Why was Seymour the wrong person?" wondered Julia. "You may not like him as much as you like Irwin, but you've made a pretty weak case against him. Some people are allergic to birds, after all. And so what if he stretched the truth a little? Who hasn't? As for learning my lesson, I think I've actually left *too much* up to destiny. Why should destiny choose *my* husband?" She reached for her history books.

Her mother looked in. "Julia, hurry and get ready! Enrollment has closed, and the contest is starting in twenty minutes. And here's another lovely treat—Mimi has helped your father with some last-minute details and will stay to watch, and even Murgatroyd-Liza has agreed to stick around for some of it, although she has her own wedding to attend. Isn't that generous of her?"

"Very warmhearted," said Julia. But when her mother had gone, she made a face at Richard. "Ha! Murgatroyd-Liza would do anything to gloat more about winning Seymour away from me. Well, all I can say is she'd better watch her back. Until they're actually married, it's still any-body's game. I'll think of something yet." She touched up her lipstick, put Richard on her shoulder, and joined her family in the hall where, with much bickering, they got in line and proceeded out to the coliseum.

As they took their places in the royal box, Julia looked glumly down at the thousand heroes on spirited steeds who lined the field, wearing armor designed by Mortimer.

Each one was probably some princess's dream, gritty, brash, and full of spirit. Yet in her view, they all lacked some quality—dignity, honor, grace, natural style, or strawberry-blond curls—that Seymour had in unfair abundance. Murgatroyd-Liza's smug smile implied that she, too, saw nobody who could come close to him. Once a girl had met a true hero, Julia thought, nobody else would do. Could destiny really mean for her to marry one of these lesser champions?

"Think!" she told herself, clasping the sides of her head.

"I do so hate public speaking," King Virgil was complaining to Queen Marianne under his breath. "I'm better at one-on-one conversation."

"Just imagine that the heroes are your devoted wife, gazing worshipfully at you during a candlelit dinner, and you'll be fine," said Queen Marianne.

The king sighed, cued the trumpets, and stood up. "Good evening, sweetheart," he called to the contestants, who jumped. Then he glared at the queen. "That was a terrible idea."

"I didn't mean for you to take it literally," said the queen. "But maybe you'd better scrap it."

The king nodded. "Yes, I think so." He turned, embarrassed, back to the heroes, and cleared his throat. "Er, I suppose you'd like to know what the challenge is now. Some of you may know me as one half of the world-famous advice team, Virgil and Marianne. If so, then you already know that I believe in poetic justice. I've designed an unconventional contest, but rest assured that it will identify the one man among you who truly loves—and thus deserves—Julia. My stewards are passing out slippery socks, knitted from the smoothest wool from the sleekest sheep in the land and heavily waxed. The landscaping team is removing the grass from the stadium floor to reveal—solid ice beneath! A midsummer miracle

courtesy of my estranged older daughter, Mimi, the cruelest witch in the entire Witchy Woods. Er," he corrected himself, with a guilty look at Murgatroyd-Liza, who was obviously fuming at the slight, "that is, one of the two cruelest witches. *Both* my older girls are as evil as the youngest is good." Murgatroyd-Liza looked slightly mollified. "Ahem, so, as I was saying, you'll race on this ice—three miles in all, six times around—wearing these socks."

The contestants immediately began paging through textbooks, cracking magic nuts, and consulting enchanted hand-mirrors. They'd all heard enough about tournaments to know that there was always a simple trick to them, which only the true hero knew, and that the person who figured it out would win.

Julia stared at her father in disbelief. She'd guessed the trick even before he'd finished speaking. "That's not even slightly impossible. *I* could win," she thought irritably.

Just then, over the crest of a distant hill, a strawberry-blond knight appeared on horseback, shimmering like a mirage.

"Oh, good—that's probably the true hero," exclaimed King Virgil, taking out his enrollment notebook. "In my day they always galloped in at the last minute, although they never cut it quite this close. What do you think, Julia? Should we let him in?"

Julia jumped to her feet and strained to look, her hand on her heart. Was it Seymour? It could be no other! As he rode closer, and his cragginess became obvious, the whole stadium began to flutter with feminine interest, while the other heroes groused about fairness and respect for other people's schedules. Julia couldn't resist a glance at Murgatroyd-Liza. What a cool customer! Her heart must be breaking at her love's betrayal, but she actually managed to look bored as Seymour galloped into the center of the ring, waving his helmet at the crowd.

Julia smiled in radiant welcome, but he didn't see her. He was busy doing a handstand on the saddle, followed by a series of backflips. The more loudly the crowd cheered, the more tricks he did. He ignored the king's attempts to find out his name and qualifications, or maybe he just couldn't hear them over his heroic whooping.

"Yawn. It's getting old, buddy," muttered Murgatroyd-Liza after about ten minutes of this. "What a show-off."

Julia had been getting a little impatient, too—it was *her* tournament, after all, and he hadn't even looked at

her yet—but her sister's blunt words rubbed her the wrong way. "I guess you're not too sorry he's broken the engagement, if that's what you think of him," she said.

"What? Him!" crowed Murgatroyd-Liza. "You thought I was talking about *that* overconfident attention-seeker? No, thanks. You're welcome to him. That isn't *my* idea of a true hero."

Julia was sure her sister was bluffing. "Well, who is this dream catch, then? He couldn't possibly be more splendid than Seymour."

"Maybe not as large or as good-looking, no," admitted Murgatroyd-Liza. "But at least he's not so self-involved. He's kind and attentive. He doesn't really get my jokes yet, but he's . . ." Searching for the right word, Murgatroyd-Liza stared off into space. "He's"—suddenly she frowned and squinted at something in the distance, and a bolt of lightning shot through her hair—"over there?"

Julia turned. Another figure had appeared over the crest. This one, even from a distance, looked much stouter than Seymour, and his stallion was small and fat.

"Oh! Well, maybe that's the true hero, then," said the king, turning a page in his notebook. "Although in my day no hero would have been caught dead on a mule. Things just aren't what they used to be."

"Irwin! What are you doing?" screeched Murgatroyd-Liza, her hair now the hub of an electric storm.

"Irwin?" repeated Julia, glancing in amazement at Richard.

"Irwin?" asked Richard. He clapped a wing over his beak. But luckily nobody heard him in all the excitement.

"Everybody calm down!" yelled the flustered king. "Young man, rein in your stallion! Sit down, Julia! Murgatroyd-Liza, turn your hair off!"

"But, Dad!" protested Murgatroyd-Liza.

"I'm still your father, and I demand order in this coliseum at once!" The king, who'd spent his whole life being sentimental, had never raised his voice before, and the surprise made everybody obey him. Even Murgatroyd-Liza sat down, her hair crackling, and the entire audience got guilty expressions and began using their library voices. Only Seymour kept riding around the ring, his horse's hooves thundering across the ice, until finally he noticed the lack of cheers and came to a puzzled stop.

Just at this moment Irwin plodded in through the entrance on the overworked mule. He was trying to be as

unobtrusive as possible, but it was difficult because the entire audience was staring at him, and his mule's dainty footfalls sounded like thunder in the complete silence. "Trust me," he thought, "to enter at the least opportune moment."

"That's better," said the king, trying not to look amazed at how effectively he'd gotten control of things. "Now, will the two latest contestants please state your names and qualifications. We'll start with you—the splendid one."

"Oh, my, no," said Seymour modestly. "I'm not a contestant."

The crowd looked crushed, and muffled sobs could be heard among the teenage girls. In the general despair, nobody noticed Julia stand up and slip out the back of the royal box with Richard on her shoulder and a determined expression on her face.

"I'm afraid I can't be persuaded," said Seymour, raising a hand. "I'm only here as an escort to the true hero, my good friend Irwin."

"The guy on the mule?" asked the crowd.

"Let's not be snide," put in King Virgil, "until we find out more about him. You claim to be a hero, young man?"

"Er," said Irwin, "I'm . . . uh . . . well, I guess, if I'm

going to be completely honest, I should admit that I couldn't get into the Heroic Academy."

The crowd spluttered with laughter. "Who can't get into that place?" somebody shouted. "I was accepted, and I'm an outright coward!"

Quentin and the other professors, who *had* lowered their standards in recent years to attract more paying students, exchanged shamefaced glances.

Seymour cleared his throat warningly and turned to the king. "Your Majesty, there's no need to dwell on the past," he said. "A briar hedge up north has positively identified him as a hero, and what's more, he loves . . ." For the first time since he'd arrived, Seymour looked for the princess. His eyes flicked past the king, the queen, Mimi, and Murgatroyd-Liza, who was incandescent with fury. He blinked. He gulped. "Er, as I was saying . . . er, he loves your beautiful daughter—"

"Goodness gracious," King Virgil interrupted him. "Marianne, do you have a spare notebook? Look at what's coming! I guess galloping in at the last moment has become very popular, and these contestants are all obviously quite certain of their chances, judging from how much luggage they've brought. What an administrative headache!"

Over the crest of the hill hundreds of figures on horseback could be seen, many laden with household appliances and leading barnyard animals behind them.

Dragging his eyes away from Murgatroyd-Liza, Seymour turned to look, too. "Those aren't contestants. They're the populace of Irwin's kingdom. Their assets are a bit liquid at the moment, since they've been forced to abandon their homes, but otherwise they're a top-notch populace. . . ." His explanation faltered, and he passed a hand over his brow. "You know, I think I'd like to enter the contest after all."

The crowd went wild. Seymour turned to Irwin apologetically. "I hate to do this to you, but I see now that you weren't kidding about Julia. She really has changed. She barely looks like the same person. I came here with every intention of leaving the field clear for you, but, well, I don't know what's come over me. I've never felt this way before. She's exquisite! I *must* win her hand."

Irwin nodded, trying to hide his disappointment. He'd done his best, but destiny obviously had other plans. He couldn't have won, after all, and if he had to see Julia marry another, at least it would be the person she loved. "I knew you'd feel differently about her once you saw her again," he said. "But where is she? I can't see her myself." He peered after Seymour's trembling finger. To his shock, Murgatroyd-Liza glowered back at him just beyond the tip of it. "Oh, no!" he croaked. "That's my fiancée!"

Seymour looked puzzled. "But your fiancée is a witch."

"Exactly," whispered Irwin.

"You mean that knockout's not Julia? Then why is she sitting with the king? And where *is* Julia?"

"I don't know," said Irwin miserably. "But I hope she doesn't see this pathetic end to my unimpressive story. Why couldn't I have sent her a letter? No, I had to prove my love in person and now I've doomed everyone"—he gestured to the Couscous populace, who were making their way into the bleachers, pack animals and all—"to Murgatroyd-Liza's fearsome vengeance. Oh, no! Here it comes! Duck!"

For the sky had darkened, and an ear-splitting shriek rang through the air.

Chapter 19

"Pardon me," said Murgatroyd-Liza as the audience turned terrified faces to her. "I've been bottling up that sneeze for a good five minutes. Dad, I hate to interrupt the tournament, but there's obviously some misunderstanding. Irwin is *my* fiancé. I'll put up with a little flirting, but competing for somebody else's hand on our wedding day is really not cool." She floated down to the coliseum floor and alit in front of the cowering Irwin. "It'll only take a few minutes," she called to the crowd with a bright smile. "Just a little lovers' spat!"

Then she turned ferociously to Irwin. "You must really like fearsome vengeance," she hissed.

"No, I don't," he protested.

Murgatroyd-Liza looked taken aback. "Well, of course not. Nobody does. I didn't really think you did. It was a veiled threat, silly. You're sort of literal-minded, aren't you?"

As Irwin tried to think of an answer, a strange noise caught his attention. He glanced at Seymour, who was actually giggling for the first time in years. "Sorry," he managed. "It's just, I didn't know witches were so funny."

"I'm glad you're tickled," said Irwin testily. "I guess the threat of fearsome vengeance has made me lose my sense of humor. Murgatroyd-Liza, if you really must wreak vengeance on somebody, please spare the citizens of Couscous. I'm the one who crossed you."

Murgatroyd-Liza was giving Seymour a sidelong glance. Nobody had ever laughed at anything she'd said before, and she couldn't tell if he was making fun of her or not. "Hmmm?" she asked Irwin.

"I said, please wreak your fearsome vengeance on me," repeated Irwin.

"Wow. That's the first time I've ever gotten *that* request," said Murgatroyd-Liza, raising her eyebrows at Seymour, who doubled up with laughter. "Don't you think we could try something else first? There's always couples' counseling."

"Stop, please!" gasped Seymour.

"For the last time, Murgatroyd-Liza, we're not a couple," said Irwin. "I would like to be your friend, but if that's not good enough for you, then please don't leave me in this suspense any longer. Hurry up with the vengeance."

Murgatroyd-Liza leaned in a little closer and spoke in a low voice. "Look, I know I threaten everybody with vengeance, but I actually don't mean anything by it. Between you and me, I'm not that good at witchcraft. The only thing I can do to you is turn you into an animal, and most victims find that rather pleasant, so if you're looking for fearsome— Oh! I have an idea. I could make you lunch sometime. My cooking is a punishment in itself."

"Punishment!" spluttered Seymour. "You're hilarious!"

"Wait till you try my ham salad," said Murgatroyd-Liza dryly, provoking a fresh outburst. "I'm Murgatroyd-Liza, by the way."

"What a lovely name," said Seymour, taking her hand and gazing at her without any flint in his eyes at all. "And I would love to try that salad sometime."

Something changed in Murgatroyd-Liza's eyes, too, as she looked back at him.

"I have to say it's not very nice of you two to be making small talk about ham salad when some people are waiting to find out what their punishments will be," said Irwin.

Murgatroyd-Liza rolled her eyes. "I'm enjoying a conversation with this young man, Irwin. Just because you don't know how to relax, you don't have to spoil everybody else's fun, too."

Irwin was hurt. "If you think I'm no fun, why do you want to marry me?"

"I'm not sure I do," she snapped back.

"Ooooo," said the audience admiringly.

Murgatroyd-Liza looked around, pleased. "In fact," she added, "I think it's time we both admitted that it's just not going to work out."

"That's telling him!" the crowd cheered.

"You're breaking up with me?" asked Irwin.

"I'm afraid so. Try not to look so excited, okay?" she added in an undertone. "I'm doing my best to save face here."

"So are you enrolling in the tournament or not?" called King Virgil, his pen poised over the notebook.

"If possible, yes," said Irwin in a dazed voice. A steward handed him a pair of waxed socks.

"And what about you?" King Virgil asked Seymour.

"I've always found ham to be the most romantic of the cured meats," Seymour was murmuring to Murgatroyd-Liza. "What?" he asked, jumping guiltily to attention. "Oh. That's okay. You boys go ahead without me."

This time the crowd, touched by the unexpected romance between the hero and the witch, seemed reconciled.

"Well, then, we might as well start," said King Virgil. "I don't know where Julia's gone, but we can't wait for her all day. After this, we have an entire wedding to get

169

through before nightfall. Heroes, please take your places at the starting line."

The other heroes hurried over, rubbing enchanted oils and powders into their socks. Irwin lined up with them.

"Irwin, wait!" cried Seymour. "You don't have a trick! You'll fall flat on your back."

"Let me help," said Murgatroyd-Liza. "I could turn you into a polar bear for the duration of the race."

"That's okay," said Irwin. "I'd rather just play it straight."

"But then you don't have a chance," said Seymour.

"Of course I do," said Irwin. "The king said that the person who truly loved Julia would win this race. If I do, then I'll win. And if there's somebody who loves her more than I do, then he deserves her."

Seymour rolled his eyes. "Irwin, remember the Academy tryouts. You ignored my advice, and look what happened. It's all very well to be idealistic, but in practice, you need to help destiny out a little. These heroes want to win just as much as you do. They're bigger and stronger and more experienced than you are, and they're not above strategizing."

"But did any of them make Murgatroyd-Liza's briar hedge bloom?" asked Irwin.

"Er," said Murgatroyd-Liza awkwardly. "I'm afraid I wasn't completely straightforward with you about the briar hedge. It was set to go off when *anybody* hacked at it. Programming it to recognize true heroes would have been too complicated. . . . Oh, dear." Irwin looked so dejected that she stopped and patted him rather awkwardly on the shoulder. "If it's any consolation, *I* mistook you for a true hero when we met." She looked guiltily at Seymour. "Of course, I was younger then—had a lot of growing up to do. . . ."

"Oh, for heaven's sakes," snapped the king, peering off into the distance at yet another figure galloping toward the stadium. "Don't they teach punctuality anymore? In my day it was an essential part of heroism. On the other hand I do like the looks of this latest contestant—now *that's* what I call a suit of armor."

The heroes glanced at each other in surprise, for the newcomer's armor was old-fashioned, gaudy, and over-decorated. He wore a raven on his shoulder, an accessory that had also gone out of style years before. His head flopped from side to side as he dismounted, walked up to the starting line, and put on his socks so clumsily that it was obvious his eyesight was very poor indeed. He didn't respond to the friendly greetings of the heroes near him at the starting line. "Must be one of those guys who's slept for a hundred years," somebody guessed. "Either that or a monster in disguise."

"Name?" asked the king.

"Sir Bildungsroman," said the knight. "From the kingdom of Ffff." He sprinkled some salt on his socks.

"Salt!" the other contestants cried in chagrin. It was so simple that none of them had thought of it. And now it was too late.

"That name sounds familiar," said Seymour. "Do we know him, Irwin?" But Irwin was despondently testing the ice with one waxy toe.

"On your mark! Get set! Go!" cried the king.

The heroes took off. Although their tricks didn't give them a lot of momentum, at least they stayed upright, lurching, gliding, and hovering gingerly over the ice. But with Irwin's first step, his socks whizzed out from under him and he found himself staring at the sky. He struggled to right himself, only to be knocked down when the heroes skated past again and again—six times in all.

"Sir Bildungsroman takes it by a nose!" shouted the referee.

Hushed excitement fell over the coliseum.

With a slow squeak, the golden armor opened, and the princess Julia stepped out.

Chapter 20

"Ha!" Julia exclaimed to the bewildered crowd. "I did it! Look, Daddy, I know it's not traditional for a princess to win her own tournament, but I just couldn't sit back and let destiny decide such an important matter for me. Now, it seems only fair that I should get to choose my fiancé. Notice that I don't say husband, because I want a long engagement. Of course, I know I can't command the person I select to marry me. He may be involved with somebody else." She glanced nervously at Margatroyd-Liza. "But he may just have gotten involved with this other person because he didn't know exactly how much I've always loved him. Once he knows, he can make his own decision. The man I would like to marry is—"

"Hold on a minute, Julia. Who says you've won?" asked the king, folding his arms.

Julia looked around in confusion. "But I came in first."

"True—but you cheated," said the king. "I saw you salting your socks. You're disqualified."

"Then I win!" cried the runner-up, Leopold.

"Nope," said the king. "*You* used pickling spice on *your* socks."

"I was just being resourceful," argued Leopold.

"If you were being resourceful, then I was being resourceful," Julia pointed out.

"Call it whatever you like," said the king. "I didn't ask you to run the race wearing salted socks, or pickled socks, or socks coated with tar or gum arabic or envelope glue. I didn't ask you to get your fairy godparents to design special toe rings or heel spikes. No, I asked you to run on ice wearing slippery socks—which is impossible, as you were all cunning enough to figure out—and the only contestant who did what I asked is right there." And he pointed to Irwin, who had resumed his hapless struggle to stand up. "Take off your socks, young man, and rise!"

It didn't occur to Irwin that the king might be talking to him. He continued to scrabble around for a good two

175

minutes while everybody waited. Eventually a hero standing near him got his attention.

"Hey!" he whispered. "Get up! You won!"

"Ha, ha," said Irwin. It was nice of this guy to try to joke around with him, but he was too disappointed to have much of a sense of humor.

"I'm serious. You're the champion!"

"Right, right. And you're the queen of Couscous, I suppose," said Irwin.

"But, Daddy!" cried Julia. "That's—that's Irwin!" She hurried over to help him up. "He's the one I wanted to marry all along!"

"He is?" asked the entire stadium.

"He is?" asked Seymour and Murgatroyd-Liza.

"I am?" asked Irwin.

"Yes—only I didn't know it until just now, when I saw you over the crest of the hill. I realized how much courage and effort it must have taken for you to get here, and how much you must care about me. And suddenly I saw that all these years what I believed was love for Seymour was just infatuation. You were the one who made me laugh, the one I could talk to, the one who listened to my childish ideas about leadership, and—*oof*!"

She dropped suddenly to the ground under the weight of a white-haired gentleman in livery.

"Pardon me," said a transformed Richard, standing and helping her up with a gloomy but practiced flourish. "Evidently somebody has fallen in love with me." He glared around at the crowd. "I hope you're happy, whoever you are." He broke down in tears.

Julia noticed that several of the heroes' steeds had also vanished, leaving perplexed-looking young men in

their places. She gasped. "Richard, it's not that somebody fell in love with you—it's that Mugatroyd-Liza herself has fallen in love, and all her spells are ending."

"Well, congratulations," Richard told the witch crossly, "but can't you turn me back into a raven?"

"Hmmm?" said Murgatroyd-Liza. Her skin was no longer quite as vivid a green as before—although it would retain an attractive lime tinge for the rest of her life. "I suppose I could try." She raised her hands above her head, then lowered them with an apologetic shake of her head. "Nope, no dice. I'm too happy to cast spells."

"Maybe Mimi could help," said Julia, turning to the royal box to look for her oldest sister—but Mimi wasn't there.

"She said something about having lived a lie for too long," said her mother, "and promised she'd be back before dinner."

"You'll have to wait until then, Richard," said Julia apologetically.

Chapter 21

That evening the populaces of Coriander and Couscous came together in a great feast to celebrate the engagements of Julia and Irwin, Murgatroyd-Liza and Seymour. The only guests who didn't seem amazed by the outcome of the tournament, or even the least bit surprised, were Irwin's parents. They claimed that the manual had predicted every moment of it, down to the socks.

"But even without the manual," Gregor told his son, "we always knew you'd do great things in life. We're very proud of you, although we'll certainly miss you at the shop."

"Maybe I could still work for you part-time," said Irwin, "on weekends, at least. Julia will be running the kingdom of Couscous, where I expect to be no more than a figurehead."

"Oh, no," said Julia. "I've been running this kingdom since I was eleven years old, and now it's your turn. Once I've trained Murgatroyd-Liza and Seymour to rule Coriander, I'll embrace my new role in Couscous as an old-fashioned queen. I'll take up embroidery and provide a traditional upbringing for the three daughters we'll have. Naturally we'll lose the first two to witchcraft, but the third will be our pride and joy, and I want to give her all the attention I never got. No daughter of *mine* will end up running around the kingdom in stolen armor or racing for her own hand in marriage."

Irwin knew that many liberal young people grew conservative as they aged, but he was surprised by the suddenness of the change in Julia. On the other hand, she'd always been precocious. "You'll give me advice, though, won't you?" he asked, nervously searching his pocket for caramels.

"Oh, advice is the last thing you'll need," she said. "The wise men will give you more than you can handle."

"The wise men!" cried Irwin, turning pale and eating several caramels at once. "They already think I'm a fool.

I was counting on you to do all
the talking around them."

"You'll find a way to manage
them, dear," said Julia. "Your
only problem is that you don't
give yourself enough credit. But

you always rise to a challenge. I remember you once
warned me that you'd never impress me, and look what
happened. You turned out to be the true hero, who
impressed me more than anybody else in the world."

"Well, I can assure you that I'll never do it again," said
Irwin gloomily, reaching for more caramels.

At this moment Mimi came in holding none other
than the perfect hero, Mortimer, by the hand. "Mortimer
and I have been dating for years, ever since the day he
tried to beat me back into the woods and ended up
staying for hors d'oeuvres," she explained. "But we both
thought getting married would damage our careers, since
heroes and witches are supposed to be sworn enemies.
Now that Seymour and Murgatroyd-Liza have broken
the ice, we don't have to hide our love anymore."

"What a relief," added Mortimer. "I can finally explain
to all those princesses that I'm already taken."

Richard hurried up to Mimi. "So love didn't stop *you* from casting spells?"

Mimi gave her sister a smug glance. "That's right. *I* kept working eight hours a day, doing terrible mischief, through the worst case of lovesickness the witch doctor had ever seen. See, Murgatroyd-Liza? *I'm* the one who's really able to balance my love life and my career."

Before Murgatroyd-Liza could get out her snide rejoinder, Richard cried, "Great! Then would you mind turning me into a raven?"

"I guess not," said Mimi. She raised her arms.

"Er, a talking raven, please," put in Richard. "And it *is* nice to have hands, I realize. I missed hands. I'd give up flying for hands. So a talking raven with hands. And no beak, please. I've never liked birdseed, and it's much easier to chew caramels with teeth."

Mimi looked taken aback. "If you don't like having wings or a beak, then why do you want to be a raven?"

"Oh, well, it's the hours, really," said Richard. "I like to set my own schedule."

"Pardon me, did you say you liked caramel?" asked Irwin's father, Gregor. "We still need somebody to take over the shop. You could be your own boss."

Richard brightened a little. "That might be a nice way to make a living," he said.

At that, the orchestra began to play, and all the couples, new and old, crowded the dance floor, where they waltzed until morning.

A few days later Mimi and Mortimer hit the road. Murgatroyd-Liza and Seymour were married and took over the Kingdom of Coriander. Once Julia felt satisfied with their performance, she and Irwin got married, too, and moved to Couscous. She stuck by her resolve to let Irwin make all the decisions, even when they seemed foolish (which they often did). To keep busy, she began writing fanciful stories based on their lives, which were eventually published (you've nearly finished reading one of them). By the time King Pignoli died and left them the kingdom, they were expecting their first child—and nobody doubted that it would be a girl.

The Heroic Academy closed its doors for lack of funds, the Heroic Certification Board disbanded, and for a time it seemed that the great era of adventure was truly over. But inevitably the world became more perilous and cruel, and young men began to right wrongs again, most of them without any training at all.

Richard made the candy shop into a profitable enterprise. His most loyal customer was King Irwin of Couscous, to whom he mailed large packages weekly. If you looked at Richard, you would never have guessed that he'd spent many years as a bird. But every once in a while, for old times' sake, he climbed a tree.